BLOOD OF BEASTS

GENESHIFTERS BOOK ONE

REBECCA LEMKE

Library of Congress Control Number: 2021921241

First Edition, November 2021

Summary: After the secret of her genetic experimentation is exposed to her best friend James, Titania is forced to flee from everything she has ever known. They must fight to stay together as they escape from the evil scientist who created her.

ISBN 978-0-9990593-2-6 (paperback) / 978-0-9990593-3-3 (hardback)

[1. Genetic engineering—Fiction. 2. Adventure and adventurers—Fiction. 3. Science fiction.]

Book Layout © 2021 BookDesignTemplates.com

Book Cover Design by Deranged Doctor Design

This book is dedicated to my husband, who has tirelessly supported me in all of my efforts, this book included.

Do you know what hurts so very much? It's love. Love is the strongest force in the world, and when it is blocked that means pain. There are two things we can do when this happens. We can kill that love so that it stops hurting. But then of course part of us dies, too. Or we can ask God to open up another route for that love to travel.

—CORRIE TEN BOOM

CHAPTER ONE

"After her!" Silen screamed at the guards.

Debris rained down on him. That blasted girl had taken out a wall! What remained of it was ablaze.

The guards scrambled to get to their feet and obey his order. Silen's vision blurred as he struggled to look toward the door. The girl's tantrum had blasted everything in the room, sending everyone flying on their backs onto the ground.

Silen still lay on the floor, blood covering his chest. The smell of burning flesh gagged him. He squirmed, trying to get away from it. He watched the guards fumble out of the collapsing room to chase after her. The titanium shackles that had held her to the wall lay in pieces on the floor. None of the other Titans had ever broken titanium shackles.

And now this one, his strongest creation, was gone.

He had known this new DNA would work, he just hadn't known it would work that well! If he could perfect more Titans like this one, there would be no doubt that the United States would be secure. No more fighting with pesky invasion threats and underhanded tactics… they would be feared. Respected. These Titans would be not only a symbol of strength, but a show of it. And he would be the genius behind it all. The thought made him giddy!

His head spun.

Silen groaned as he struggled to right himself. He willed his body to sit up. Silen had no faith in his guards. He wanted to go after her himself.

This one was truly powerful. Dangerously perfect.

She couldn't be on the loose. She'd ruin everything.

It had all happened so fast. Just moments before, he'd been in her face. Harassing her.

Taunting her with the nickname Titania, if only she could break the shackles.

He'd only meant to get her riled up enough for the integration to take. It had worked.

Silen stood, gingerly placing his hand on the now bent medical tray table to stabilize himself. He said a silent prayer as he searched for the tracker. Even if the guards let her go, he should be able to find her with it. If she had broken it—no, he refused to consider the possibility. That tracker was his only hope.

The ceiling groaned. The fire licked at it, impatient to devour.

He searched the scattered remains of the lab, turning over smoldering pieces of drywall.

"Ah," he said as he brushed aside the bent needle he'd used to inject her. "There you are."

He held the tracker before him, grinning at it as a green light blinked weakly back at him.

He rushed out the door. A huge chunk of burning rafter narrowly missed him as the room caved in behind him.

"You won't escape me," Silen promised.

"I'll find you."

TEN YEARS LATER

James paced outside the fence of the Lone Leaf compound, back straight and tall. A few people lingered inside the caged yard, but most had left the enclosed wire dome for the evening.

He kept his eyes alert and focused on the perimeter, save for the glances he stole at Titania. Her brown hair hung in wisps in front of her eyes. She didn't bother tucking them away.

He could tell something was troubling her. Although she appeared to be alert, acting as though she was scanning between the nearby woods and the tall dome that enclosed the yard of the compound, he could see that her mind was somewhere else.

She slouched beneath the weight of the backpack she was carrying.

"What do you even have in that thing?" he asked incredulously.

"Huh?" she responded, her head snapping up to look at him.

James pointed to the backpack and raised an eyebrow.

"Nothing," Titania said, jutting her chin up at him.

"Nothing looks awfully heavy," he teased.

She stuck her tongue out at him like a petulant child. He smirked, enjoying the rise he had gotten out of her.

The sunset shone in their eyes, turning Titania's irises to a liquid honey color as they headed around the corner of the fence and toward the West. James held his hand up to shield his own eyes for better visibility. They had more privacy here, in the blind spot of the cameras attached to the building. And it was outside of the range of people hearing them from the yard.

Now was his chance.

He wanted to talk about them. About their future. They did in the abstract often, but with his recent sixteenth birthday, he wanted to talk about it in a more concrete way.

"I—" James began.

Titania tensed, causing the words to die in his throat. Had he startled her again?

He followed her gaze to the edge of the woods. Seeing nothing, he continued.

"I was wondering," he began again, but she held up a hand to stop him.

Titania held a finger to her lips, instructing him to be quiet.

The unspoken words crawled back down his throat and died of suffocation. Part of him was angry he didn't keep trying, but the other part was still scared to bring it up to her. Titania crept toward the woods, hands buried in the pockets of her dark hoodie. He followed wordlessly behind her. She was his best friend. He would always follow her, even if it was just to get her out of the trouble she created.

"What are we doing?" he whispered.

Titania glared back at him.

He tried to hide it, but he couldn't help but smirk, which always made her even more mad at him.

She whipped around, her brown waves dancing in the breeze.

They reached the edge of the woods. Titania looked back at the compound, checking to make sure no one was watching. She stepped beyond the trees and into the forest. James shook his head, disappearing in after her.

He followed her to a tree just outside of the view of the compound. If anyone tried to follow them or inquire of their whereabouts, they could always say they had heard a noise and went to investigate. Goodness knew, the older guys who did patrol duty snuck off to smoke all the time. The patrol was so everyone inside felt trapped, not safe. They all knew that, even if some chose to ignore it.

James watched Titania sit down and slide the backpack off. He crouched beside her as she opened it up.

Before he could question what she was doing, something caught his attention in his peripheral vision.

A small human face peeked out at them from behind a tree about eight feet further into the forest. James' eyes widened in surprise.

"Titania..." he whispered.

Several more faces appeared from behind the trees, all of them very young and frail-looking.

Titania paid him no mind as she pulled out food from her bag. Protein bars manufactured within the compound, genetically modified fruits and vegetables, and even a few containers of dried meat. He knew how she had gotten these; she worked in the hydroponics area of the compound. But how had she snuck them out without being noticed?

James grimaced. Knowing her, it was possible she might not have. But there were a few higher-ups that seemed to have a bizarre sweet spot for her. It wasn't that she was bulletproof, and she didn't test that theory all that often, but James had noticed it, nonetheless. People seemed to either love her or hate her, with no in between. He hoped that if they had noticed her stealing food, they wouldn't send her away. She was still only fifteen, so she'd be sent into the wilds rather than a delinquent compound if they caught her with a charge that severe. The government wouldn't waste resources on a traitor that was about to age out.

The children emerged and began walking toward them as Titania put the food on a fallen log in front of her. James' heart twinged as he looked at the kids. Their bones were uncomfortably visible.

Food wasn't plentiful, especially for those of the lower classes. So much of the land was barren. It wasn't safe to use for crops anymore because of radiation poisoning and years of chemical warfare, but it had been unusable long before that. Nobody knew why. One day, the crops just stopped growing. The farmers and homesteaders tried to stay and continue to make a go of things, but they had all died out trying. Even now, some of the remaining vestiges of civilization outside of compounds tried to utilize the accursed fields, but they didn't last very long after doing so. It made James wonder how these people could even survive in the wild. By the looks of these kids, he suspected maybe most didn't.

Titania smiled at him as the children rushed on the food and split it amongst themselves. They devoured it right then and there. An older girl grabbed an extra portion and gave it to a toddler she had sitting on her hip.

The toddler seemed lethargic to James, even the bites of dried fruit didn't seem to perk it up. He stepped forward, intending to ask if there was something wrong. He had been trained as a medic. Maybe he could help and provide the child some medicine. But the girl spooked and turned to bolt.

Titania stood up to calm her, but it was no use. The children scattered into the woods, food in hand. James felt bad, he hadn't intended to scare them.

"It's okay," Titania said, nodding to James, "They aren't used to people who aren't trying to hurt them."

James nodded. He knew the government didn't take kindly to people who didn't fall in line. And if they were living outside a compound, that was a sure sign they didn't.

"How long have you been taking them food?" James asked. "How many are there?"

"A few months, maybe," Titania admitted. "There are fewer each time."

"That baby…"

"Won't be here next time," Titania cut him off.

There was a silence that fell over them as she zipped up the backpack.

"You're risking a lot by bringing them food," James stated, running his hands nervously through his dark hair.

"I'm risking even more if I don't," Titania said defiantly.

James sighed. He closed the space between them, staring down at her.

"I have the ability to do what's right," Titania growled. She pointed a finger back at the compound beyond the edge of the woods. "And if I don't, I'm no better than them."

James looked down at her, his eyes trailing down to her hand. He knew if he took it in his, she would pull away. She acted like she wanted to be together, but anytime she felt like he was getting too close, she withdrew. It had always been that way. He never understood it. He knew she expected him to bristle at what she had said. To argue with her. To explain to her what a rational person would do to protect themselves. But he didn't feel like fighting. He chewed on his lip, taking his frustration out on it.

"I love you," he said simply, surprising even himself.

There it was, out in the open. His heart pounded in his chest, blood rushing in his ears. It drowned out any sense he had left.

Before she could respond, he wrapped his arms around her. He could feel her warmth, smell the earthiness of the woods her hair had soaked up, and count every single beat of her wild heart.

She froze at first, then seemed to lean into him for a brief second before pulling away. Her eyes were wide with fright.

"I'm sorry," James apologized. That had not been the reaction he was hoping for.

"No," Titania absolved him, "I'm sorry. It's not you, I was just… surprised."

James rubbed the back of his neck, admittedly feeling confused and rejected.

"I promise, I won't do any more surprises."

CHAPTER THREE

Pain. Sheer pain.

It erupted within her the moment he had touched her. The burning sensation of every piece of nerve, flesh, and bone.

She stepped back, pulling away from him before it consumed her entirely. Titania looked into his eyes, pools of sea green. She felt lost in them, just as she did in much of life.

James was hurt. She knew he was. She knew he didn't understand.

But it had to be this way. Someday, she'd tell him. Just not today.

Titania tugged at the sleeves of her hoodie as they walked back to the compound, pulling it down over her burnt skin. She was thankful the garment was thick and fluffy.

Titania stole a glance at James, hoping he hadn't noticed. Nothing in his face indicated that he had, but she caught him looking at her.

He looked away, scurrying over to the gate of the fence to let her in.

"After you," James said, holding the door open.

She stepped in begrudgingly, hating to leave the freedom outside. They were back inside the cage. Trapped. Her soul revolted.

The compound itself resembled a prison with a main one-story building of plain white brick construction and boarded-up windows. The outdoor yard, enclosed as it was in a cage, was mostly paved with concrete. It was easy to feel stifled by the sterility of it all.

James noticed her frustration and gave her a consoling smile. She forced herself to smile back at him in the most convincing way she could muster.

They trekked across the enclosure of the fence, passing by the picnic tables and run-down basketball court. The compound only kept a few semblances of the normalcy of the old world to improve morale. A throwback to when people could laugh and play and enjoy themselves.

It was hard to truly enjoy such things when that world was long gone. They were surrounded by chaos now.

Titania's hand curled into a fist as she dug her nails into her palm to steady herself. It helped her to focus her mind on the pain. The mounting anger at being contained again was causing the burns to spread. She felt the heat rising along her neck. If they spread too far, she wouldn't be able to hide it.

She couldn't abide that. The safety of her secret was the only touchstone she had. She could make everyone think she was normal, even herself.

James heaved a sigh as he grabbed the door handle of the compound.

"Wait," Titania said abruptly. James released it, cocking an eyebrow at her.

Titania knew he hated this just as much as she did, but he kept it together for her. He let her complain while he looked at the bright side. They balanced each other out that way. For as much as she had been robbed of normalcy between her secret and the compound, he had been, too. She may not be able to reciprocate physical affection, but she didn't want there to be a doubt in his mind about the way she felt.

"I love you too," she said. Her heart took off at breakneck speed. She grabbed the door handle, not glancing back at him to see his reaction at all. Her cheeks burned as she stepped inside. She hoped they weren't noticeably red.

One of James' friends sidled up to him as he came in behind her. The boy immediately started ribbing him.

"Y'all sure were out there a while." He lowered his voice, "Were you—?"

James cut him off with the wave of a hand before he said something uncouth, as he often did. Though the boy wasn't much younger than James, James now outranked him within the compound since he'd turned sixteen. Titania had to admit, he did look older and more put together now. Instead of t-shirts and ripped jeans, he wore button-up shirts and clean blue jeans. Titania could tell that the boy was intimidated and unsure of how to navigate the new dynamic, but aired on the side of caution.

"We noticed something in the woods, but it's taken care of now," James said in a low, threatening voice.

"Noticed something, eh?" the boy taunted and hiked his thumb toward Titania. "Oh, I bet you did…"

Titania opened her mouth to protest, but she thought better of it. If anyone was going to get into trouble tonight, it wasn't going to be her. She didn't want to give anyone a reason to search her or her backpack, especially with the fresh burns she was sporting. If they got any more intense, they might damage her clothes.

Still, she stared at the boy with contempt. She didn't care for hardly anyone at the compound except James, but some of these boys were too much.

"Is that how you talk about a lady?" James folded his arms and lengthened his spine, towering over his peer.

"Ah, man." The boy punched James in the arm nervously. "You know I was just joking with you."

James raised an eyebrow. The boy flinched and muttered an insincere apology.

"You're no fun anymore," he mumbled as he slunk away.

James, ever the patient one, let it slide. Titania sometimes wished that he'd let fewer things slide, but tonight she was grateful.

They made their way through the cafeteria, eavesdropping on conversations as they went. The easiest way to get the news was to listen to the chatter of the cafeteria at the end of the day.

A man at the end of one of the tables waved at them. James waved back at him, intending to keep moving along with Titania. But the man motioned for him to come over. James furrowed his brow.

"I'll be right back." He briefly patted her shoulder before joining the man.

Titania held her breath, waiting for the burning sensation to return. She had gotten almost all of it to go away; she didn't have the energy to do that again tonight. Titania had gotten good at hiding her flaming skin over the years, but it took its toll.

"Titania!" A young girl with fiery red hair ran up to her. "Have you heard the news?"

Titania bristled. The younger children rarely had a concept of personal space, and Abigail was no exception.

"What news?" Titania asked her, knowing she was just waiting for permission to spill.

Abigail lowered her voice rather dramatically, "You know that contamination, the kind Chris saw on the mushrooms near the woods?"

"Yeah…" Titania hesitated. "What about it?"

"It's been found in the food lab," Abigail's voice wobbled with uncertainty.

Titania looked over at James, who was fully engaged in conversation with the man at the table. She likely had time to see this for herself before they finished. Plus, she could use the time away from him to process what had just happened.

"Can you show me?" Titania looked down at Abigail.

Abigail glanced around nervously, her small frame making her jitters all the more dramatic. Titania knew she didn't want to get in trouble for spreading a rumor.

"Oh shoot," Titania said, a little louder than their conversation required, "I forgot to water the strawberries!"

Abigail looked confused for a moment, but then had to suppress a grin. She knew exactly what Titania was up to. They now had a reason to enter the food lab without raising any suspicions.

"Would you mind helping me? It'll go a lot quicker with an extra set of hands," Titania asked Abigail.

"Sure!" Abigail said, playing along.

Titania led the way down the hall to the back of the compound. Once they were out of earshot of the cafeteria, Titania spoke up.

"How bad is it?" she asked Abigail.

"I've only heard about it," Abigail said. "I don't even know if it's true."

"I guess we shall see," Titania said, pulling the keys out of her pocket.

She shoved one into the food lab door and turned it. The lock clicked. Titania pulled the door open and ushered Abigail in.

The only light in the room came from the lamps above the plants. The windows were boarded up long ago; they were too risky. If people could see in, they could see the resources the compound had and try to take them. A faint purple glow broke through the dark in the back corner of the room. Titania squinted, wondering if she was seeing things.

Abigail looked up from the plant she was inspecting and followed Titania's gaze. They wordlessly moved in unison to investigate.

Titania set her jaw as she laid eyes on the source of purple light. In an enclosed glass case lay a small, luminous onion.

The rumor was true; the contamination had breached the building.

They hadn't been able to discern what was causing this in the mushrooms in the woods. They suspected some kind of radioactivity like what now affected the fields. It certainly wasn't safe to eat. If the contamination had somehow gotten into the facility, as it seemed it had, they could lose their entire food supply.

They'd be as vulnerable to starvation or illness from these strange plants as the children that came through the woods.

Titania glanced at Abigail's wide eyes. She steeled herself, committing herself to be strong for Abigail's sake. Having the younger children panicking would only cause the situation to worsen.

"It'll be okay," Titania assured her, cursing herself for bringing Abigail along to investigate. "This is contained. The rest of the crops will be just fine."

Titania stiffened at the sound of a knock at the door. She noticed the distinctive pattern and relaxed a bit.

"It's bedtime." She put a hand on Abigail's back and led her to the door.

Titania pushed it outward and shooed Abigail back toward the cafeteria before stepping through herself. She let the door close and, even though she knew he would be behind it, James startled her.

Her breath caught. He was leaning up against the wall with his arms crossed. She couldn't help but admire him, though she knew she shouldn't under the circumstances. It was like her mind needed a reprieve, and every darkened feature of his face and frame was just the thing to make her forget that the world was ending. He was a sea of darkness in a perfect storm.

He smirked at her. Her cheeks burned with shame. She was so stupid! She should've said something instead of standing there ogling him.

"You alright there, Princess?" James asked with strangled sincerity.

"Don't call me that!" Titania protested, balling her fists up at her sides.

The keys in her hand dug into her flesh, giving her something to focus on instead of her emotions running wild.

He knew she hated it when he called her that, which gave him all the more reason to do it. He seemed to enjoy making her mad.

James laughed, breaking his pose against the wall to stand nearer to her. He moved with a grace she had never understood or been able to emulate.

"I have something to tell you," Titania said, her mind returning to the contaminated food.

"I have something to tell you too," James said, "and I expect my news is a bit more dire."

"I'd be shocked," Titania laughed dryly.

James tilted his head and nodded, encouraging her to go first.

Titania stole a glance down the hall and, finding no one watching, motioned for James to follow her into the food lab.

He trailed behind her to the corner, passing by the rows and rows of vegetables under grow lights.

She looked at the contaminated onion, then at him. The purple glow illuminated his green eyes and tanned skin. His expression was tight. He knew exactly what he was looking at. "It's inside the compound now," he said, muttering to himself.

He quickly sobered, just as she had with Abigail. Someone always had to be the stoic one, so it seemed.

James led her out, waiting patiently as she locked up.

"Titania…" he started, "there are some rumors going around…"

"About the contamination?" Titania said as they walked to the dorm hallway. "I know. That's what Abigail told me. I think we need to discourage them so we don't have a bunch of panicked people."

"No," James said, stopping in his tracks.

Titania paused and met his gaze, surprised.

"George told me that there might be riots," James explained.

"Well, what's new?" Titania said, unfazed as she started back toward the dorms again. "There are always riots."

"No," James caught up as he tried to get through to her. "Not in the cities. Here. He says there might be riots here."

Ice ran through Titania's veins. She locked eyes with James, searching for some reassurance that things would be okay. That it was just a rumor. They'd lived in this compound peaceably for almost ten years.

They were a smaller compound, which meant they weren't much of a target to nearby towns. Most of their fighting manpower had been redirected to other facilities with weapons and other more valuable commodities or people. They didn't have the resources to handle a riot, but maybe they could request reinforcements.

"When?" Titania asked, biting her lip.

James wouldn't meet her eyes.

"Soon," he said reluctantly.

They turned left down the hallway to the girl's wing.

"What are we going to do?" Titania asked, staring blankly ahead.

James stopped in front of her door. "We can talk about it more tomorrow."

His gaze flitted from her eyes, to her lips, and finally to her forehead. She felt heat climb up her neck in response. He looked as though he was going to lean in, but thought better of it at the last second.

"Goodnight Princess," he whispered.

He turned and walked away, hands in his pockets.

Titania watched him go, her heart racing. She wasn't sure what was going to kill her first, the stress or that boy.

CHAPTER FOUR

James sat in the medical bay, staring at patient paperwork. He was the last medic the compound still had, which meant he was in charge of every health crisis that arose. They didn't have much of an aging population, thankfully, but even so, he had plenty of work keeping him busy.

He flipped through the pieces of paper, mindlessly scanning them. James worried about his patients. Plenty of them were growing depressed, and who could blame them? There was plenty to be depressed about when you live in a cage and the world was ending. But James thought it might be more than that. There had been a certain resilience within the compound before. But now that they had sent a good portion of their population to other compounds, that seemed to dwindle.

He wondered if it could be because they were going into winter. The October chill in the air was keeping everyone inside, instead of out sunbathing and getting vitamin D.

James threw the papers down and stood to pace. Bones were so much easier to mend than brains, he thought.

A knock at the door rattled his thoughts. He strode over and opened it.

"Do you have a moment?" his senior officer inquired.

"Of course, Officer Adrienne," James motioned him in. "Please, take a seat."

Given that there was only a single chair and one spinning stool, the officer took the chair.

James proceeded to the stool and tried to sit in a dignified manner.

"To what do I owe this visit?" James asked. He fidgeted, moving his toes around inside his shoes so Adrienne wouldn't notice. His mind raced, wondering if someone had reported him and Titania being out late. But this could be nothing.

"I assume by now you've probably heard," Adrienne sighed. "George doesn't have a good track record of keeping his mouth shut."

James suppressed a smirk. Anything he could have said would be to have spoken out of turn, so he simply nodded an affirmative.

Adrienne rolled his eyes. "I should just use that man as a bulletin board for this place, it'd be more efficient."

James coughed to cover a laugh that slipped out.

"Well," said Adrienne, "let me get right to it then. As you know, you have the choice to transfer out when you turn sixteen—happy birthday, by the way."

"Thank you," said James.

The officer nodded in acknowledgment.

"Normally this would be as simple as me giving the choice to stay or go, and my personal recommendation. However, the situation is a lot more complicated."

The officer paused for a moment. "Riots will be here within the week, maybe within the next few days. Nobody would blame you for leaving out before that happens. It's pretty pointless to lose a good medic to an angry mob. We have so little manpower, you'd be on the front line."

"How bad is it supposed to be?" James said, his eyebrows scrunched in concern. He couldn't imagine the locals having that much manpower, but then again, nobody knew too much about life outside the compound. It was all speculation unless they gave you the clearance to know.

"We're temporarily moving the elderly and minors tomorrow afternoon to prepare."

James was dumbfounded. Did they expect the rioters to burn the place down? Sure, they didn't have the firepower of other compounds, but this seemed excessive.

"Who's going to defend the people left in the compound?" James asked.

"That's not for you to worry about," Adrienne brushed the question aside. "Your only concern right now should be deciding whether you would like to stay or go. And if you want to go, where? The Vandament facility could use more medics and is one of the most lucrative moves you could make."

James rubbed his face with his hand. Vandament was a huge deal. If he could go to Vandament right off the bat, he would be set.

This was a lot to take in. Riots were one thing. So was deciding on a place to go for career advancement. But in this scenario? He felt like he was being asked to abandon the compound and everyone inside of it for his own personal gain.

"I don't need an answer from you tonight," Adrienne said, noticing his overwhelm. "Sleep on it! Just let me know by mid-morning tomorrow, that way I can make transportation arrangements while we are moving other residents, and do it in plenty of time before the rioters arrive."

"Yes sir," James responded.

"Right," said Officer Adrienne. "I'll be off then and let you work."

James stood up to open the door for him.

A sickening thought struck him as Adrienne crossed the threshold.

"Sir," James addressed him.

The officer turned around.

"What is it?" he asked patiently.

"My friend," James explained. "She won't turn sixteen for another two months, and I…"

Adrienne put a hand up, stopping James mid-sentence.

"She'll be safe. We'll put her in the van with the other minors," Adrienne assured him with a smile.

James grimaced. "I was hoping that she could accompany me if I decided to leave. My plan was to defer my decision until she came of age. I didn't think we'd be discussing it so soon. Is it possible for her to come with me if I decide to go to Vandament?" Officer Adrienne heaved an exasperated sigh.

"I do understand, son, but that's against policy. It's possible that when she comes of age, she may be able to go to Vandament. You'd only be separated for a couple of months, that's not too bad."

"What happens if I stay?" asked James.

Adrienne's jaw tightened. James knew he was offended, but he had to ask. He had to know.

"I wouldn't recommend it. You'd be passing up the opportunity of a lifetime," Adrienne said tersely. "Is she worth that?"

James stood before him, forcing a blank expression onto his face to dissuade a lecture.

"I would hope I wouldn't need to tell you, but I urge you to use discretion with the information I've given you today. If you tell your friend that she'll be loaded with the other minors and she causes funny business, it'll come out of your hide," Adrienne said. His stern expression told James everything he needed to know.

"Yes, sir," James said, struggling against the lump building in his throat.

Adrienne grunted and strode away before James could say anything more.

James didn't usually feel like the world was ending, even though it was. But the thought of being separated from Titania was crushing. Who was going to protect her and look after her? What was he going to tell her? How could he even decide?

CHAPTER FIVE

Titania padded down the hallway from her room, turning at the end of the hall to the cafeteria. Her feet drug across the sterile white floor. In her exhausted state, she had barely bothered to comb through her hair. She picked her feet up only to avoid the irritating squeaks that resulted from the contact between her shoes and the floor.

"Sleep well, Princess?" James asked as she strode up to him. He sat at their normal spot in the corner of the cafeteria.

Titania groaned, glaring at him. He pulled a chair out for her and patted the top of it, inviting her to sit. She took it, but not without sticking her tongue out at him.

She pulled the sleeves of her shirt down over her hands and folded her arms over the table, laying her head down dramatically. She was definitely not a morning person.

Titania heard James take a sip of his coffee and let out a heavy sigh. Her mischievous smile fell away at the sound. She rolled her head to the side to look at him. His expression was tight and withdrawn. Was he mad at her? He didn't usually mind her morning grunts and groans.

His concerning demeanor prompted her to sit upright.

James didn't react to the sudden shift. Instead, he stared off into the wall, his green eyes unfocused and unblinking.

Titania cleared her throat.

"Earth to James." She waved her hand in front of his face. "Earth to James!" He flinched, shaking his head.

"What?" James said frantically. "What?"

"You a little distracted there, chief?" Titania teased to mask her concern.

"Oh," James said, coming back to the present. "Yeah, just tired."

"Did you sleep poorly?" Titania stole a glance at his full coffee mug. She didn't expect fatigue was the answer considering he had barely touched it. And the fidgeting he did with the buttons on his sleeve was a dead giveaway that he was lying.

"Yeah," James wouldn't meet her gaze. "Weird dreams."

Titania narrowed her eyes at him.

James pulled out a well-worn pack of playing cards before she could grill him any further. Her eyes lit up. He knew too well how to distract her.

Her spirits lifted as she watched his nimble hands shuffle the deck and make a bridge. He was so much better at that than she was. When they were kids, she had stayed up all night trying to learn card tricks to impress him.

James dealt the cards out between himself and Titania until they both had a pile.

"What are we playing?" Titania asked.

"I figured Egyptian Rat? Unless you want to play something else—"

"No, no," Titania grinned. "That's perfect."

James regarded her with a friendly smirk and set his first card down.

They went around and around. James took the first pile after having put down a king. Titania took a much smaller pile next. They stayed about even just on luck, which wasn't very exciting.

A few monotonous rounds in and Titania slapped her hand down on a pair of jacks. She looked at James and frowned. He hadn't even tried to get it. Playing cards wasn't any fun when his head wasn't in the game.

Titania leaned back. James had checked out, gazing at Titania's chair without actually looking at it.

"Are you going to tell me what's going on?" Titania couldn't keep the irritation from her voice. It crept in and stung him.

She could tell by the way he flinched.

James looked anywhere but at her.

"What do you think is going to happen if the contamination spreads to all of our crops?" James cast a sidelong glance at the group at the table next to him, lowering his voice.

Despite his hushed tone, his voice was clean and calm. Titania couldn't stand it. On its own, the question didn't offend her. But she knew by the way he talked that he was holding something back.

"I suppose we'll figure something out." Titania threw her hands up, then nervously combed them through her hair. "We always do."

"But what if we can't this time?" James pressed, forcing his voice down even further.

"What's the plan then?"

Titania pushed her anger down. She hated it when James played devil's advocate.

"It sounds like you have some answer to that," Titania said in exasperation. "So why don't you just come out with it?"

James looked around nervously. "I think we need to be prepared to leave—"

"LEAVE?" Titania yelped, "What do you—"

James' eyes widened as he looked out at the half-full cafeteria. He tried to hush Titania as a few people swiveled their heads toward their corner.

"We don't need to broadcast it," James chastised her with a whisper.

She crossed her arms and slumped back in her chair.

"How could you even talk like that?" Titania said, quieter this time. "This is practically all we've ever known. You don't think that's worth fighting a little biological contamination for?"

James tried to reach out, to take her hand, but she shoved her chair back out of his reach.

"We might be fighting more than just the contamination," James broached. "The riots are coming here, it's not a rumor."

"And?" Titania said. "We'll deal with them. I can't believe you would just abandon this place!"

"Don't you want to do more in life than what we can here?" James leaned across the table and asked. "Don't you want to see more of the world?"

"You really think anything outside is different from here?" Titania was incredulous. "It's all destruction, chaos, and radioactive plants. Hardly anything to write home about."

James sat back and let out a deep sigh. He drug both hands down his face before making eye contact with her.

"They have offered me the opportunity to go work at Vandament. I'd like to accept it."

The blood rushed out of Titania's face, her hands gripping the sides of her chair.

Vandament?

Vandament was a big deal. It was one of the most prestigious compounds left in the country. One that surely wouldn't need her for anything. She didn't have any kind of impressive resume or skills. All she did was care for plants, which wasn't that hard.

Which meant…

"You'd leave me?" Her words were almost inaudible.

"No," James waved his hand to dispel her concern. "No, not at all. I mean, I may have to go a couple of months ahead of you, but that's all."

Titania shook her head. "Were you even going to ask me if I wanted to go? Did you even consider that?"

"I— "

A loud boom interrupted their conversation.

"What was that?" Titania asked as she looked around.

She noticed the cafeteria was almost empty. When had everyone filed out?

James was already on his feet. Titania jumped up to follow him as he headed toward the back of the compound, nearly getting caught on her chair as it snagged her jeans.

"How long have you known about Vandament?" Titania demanded to know as she caught up to him. "Were you even going to tell me if I hadn't noticed that you were being weird?"

Another boom reverberated through the hallway before he could answer. They raced to the back door, unsure of what to expect.

"We'll talk about this later." James scowled.

Titania reached for the door handle to open it. She wanted to know what all the ruckus was about.

James put his arm out to stop her.

"Stay behind me," he instructed.

She rolled her eyes, but obeyed.

James cautiously opened the door.

CHAPTER SIX

James and Titania squinted against the brightness outside. Titania gasped.

"What is going on?" James wondered aloud as he took in the chaos.

Disheveled-looking people lined the outside of the fence, brandishing crude weapons while banging on it and shouting. They surrounded the entire cage and, from the look of it, wrapped around the sides of the building. James thought the rioters looked feral, with wild eyes, unkempt hair, and tattered clothes. A few wore strange masks with a symbol on them. Lone Leaf officers lined the inside of the cage, staring down the crowd from within. One officer herded a group of compound workers past James and Titania back inside the building.

James noticed a van idling in the middle of the cage. The back doors were hanging open. He recognized the children and a few elderly from the compound nestled inside, many of whom were crying. His brain struggled to make sense of what he was seeing. His thoughts moved like jello, slow and clumsy.

He took in a sharp breath as the realization hit him.

The riots were here. They were early. The kids were leaving right now.

"Oh, good." Officer Adrienne approached James and broke through his thoughts. "You brought her."

James' gaze followed Adrienne's extended arm to Titania standing next to him.

"Brought me?" Titania recoiled. "What is he talking about?"

James' muscles locked up, paralyzing him in place. Officer Adrienne stared him down. James knew he was being threatened. He knew the consequences for making this more difficult.

She would be safer leaving.

But as he watched Titania's eyes widen in shock from Adrienne reaching out and latching onto her, he couldn't bring himself to believe that.

She fought against Adrienne as he drug her along, taking large strides to cross the courtyard. James felt helpless as he watched Adrienne tighten his grip on Titania and rush her to the back of the van. Everything was happening so fast! She cried out in pain as Adrienne threw her in. A tear fell down her cheek as she held her arm where Adrienne had grasped it. James' blood boiled. It melted away whatever held him in place. There was no need for Adrienne to have been rough with her.

James dashed toward the van, reaching for Titania. He couldn't let this happen! He couldn't let Adrienne take her to goodness knows where. James had been wrong to even think about being separated.

He couldn't wait to tell her she had been right about that when this was all over. James would get her out of there and go back into the compound. Adrienne could deal with it. James didn't care if it ruined his chances to go to Vandament. The end of civilization was the end of civilization, regardless of whether or not it was cushier. He would rather be with Titania for that. They could come up with a plan to fend off the rioters. It would all be okay.

Titania disappeared from his view as Adrienne slammed the back of the van shut and gave a signal to the driver. The vehicle pitched forward right as James reached for the handle of the door. James peeked around to see another officer from the compound at the gate preparing to open it.

What were they going to do? Run people over? How were they going to keep rioters from running into the courtyard once the van was through?

The driver sped up as the van neared the gate and the officer dutifully pushed it open. The rioters on the other side let out a collective gasp. It rippled through their numbers as they realized the van would run them over if they didn't move.

James watched them scatter to avoid being hit. The van bobbed up as the wheels rolled over something. His stomach lurched. James averted his gaze; he didn't want to know. He'd never be able to get the image out of his head. He already had enough of them, working as a medic.

A banging from the inside of the van caught his attention. The back door swung open just as the van cleared the gate.

Titania stood, clutching her arm with a triumphant smile on her face. James watched as she bent her knees and prepared to jump. She faltered at the sight on the ground before her. James followed her gaze, against his better judgment. It was gruesome. There were bones protruding out at sickening angles.

One rioter reached for Titania. The van wasn't moving fast enough to carry her out of his range. He grabbed her by the throat, pulling her out of the van. Titania grasped at the man's hand as she writhed in the air, clawing at it with all her might. She couldn't even scream because of how tightly the man held on. James rushed toward her assailant, all inhibitions gone. He would not let her die. He could not.

"One of yours for one of ours!" the man shouted.

The rabid crowd echoed him, "One of yours for one of ours!"

The barbaric rioters worked themselves into a frenzy, beating the sides of the van as it pulled away, doors swinging wildly. They rushed into the courtyard through the open gate, attacking the officer there first. The wave of people pushed James back toward the compound.

He lost sight of Titania. James rushed through the crowd with superhuman strength and mental fortitude. He

deftly avoided getting hit by any weapons or stray punch-
es, as the cage became a fighting ring.

James reached the gate and burst through to the other
side. He glanced around, looking just above the heads of
the crowd for where the rioter might still be suspending
Titania in the air.

His guts twisted when he couldn't find her. Had the
man killed her and thrown her to the ground? The mental
image of her lifeless body, discarded on the barren earth,
filled him with unbridled rage.

A strangled, deep cry rang out. James looked around
instinctively, trying to find the source. The rioters parted
in a circle, one that surrounded the man who had grabbed
Titania. James marched toward him, his embitterment apparent on his face. The man sat on his knees, head droop-
ing toward the ground.

"Where is she?" James bellowed.

When the man didn't respond, James turned to the
crowd.

"Where is she?" he demanded, even louder than before.

He examined their faces, all perfectly painted masks
of horror. One turned to face him directly. A vacancy consumed their eyes. James faltered.

He could be intimidating, for sure. But these people
had no reason to fear him.

James examined the crowd. Some were looking at the
man kneeling on the ground, whom he presumed to be
their leader. James saw the man's hands weakly placed on

his lap. Black char marks covered them, some patches of skin were melted beyond repair.

James' eyes widened. What had done that?

He looked around, following the gaze of the other members of the crowd, straight up.

There, twenty-five feet above them, was a girl on fire. Her skin was black, like cooled lava, with sparks emitting from simmering veins of fire that ran across her body. Her clothing shriveled back here and there as the flames licked at it. Her hair was ablaze, but rather than being consumed, it remained in place, engulfed in a perpetual red flame.

Black feathered wings suspended her in the air with minimal effort. Each was slightly longer than Titania was tall, and they beat rhythmically to keep her aloft.

She grasped at her abdomen, covering it as she cradled her arms.

A tear ran down her cheek, sizzling as the heat evaporated it.

§

Titania struggled to breathe. Struggled to think. Struggled to stay above the crowd. The pain overwhelmed her.

She looked at James, making eye contact for a moment. His eyes widened. Her stomach dropped. Did he think she was a monster now? All that time, she'd kept it from him. And now he knew. She cursed herself for not just coming out with it sooner. He probably hated her now.

"Titania?" She saw his mouth move.

She looked away. Tears blurred her vision as she started losing altitude. She weakly moved her wings to steady herself.

"What kind of monsters are you keeping here?" she heard a man shout at James.

"Is this what the government is going to use to get rid of us?" another voice from the crowd piped up.

The momentary silence and morbid curiosity were over. Chaos reigned yet again as the rioters began attacking. Their cries carried into the sky, tormenting her.

She tried to keep an eye on James. She winced as he took a punch to the gut when the crowd closed in on him. She watched him pushing through the crowd of people.

Titania started to fall to the ground, her wings failing her. She had to get out of here. Maybe if she could distract the rioters, James could get away.

She saw a gnarled, middle-aged man kick James in the back of the knee, sending him tumbling to the ground.

"What?" the rioter taunted with a gravelly voice. "You don't do nothin' special like her?"

Titania's stomach churned. She didn't want anyone getting hurt on her account.

She angled her turbulent descent to the edge of the clearing. She belatedly realized that a few of the rioters who had spotted her were running toward her landing spot.

Titania landed with a thud, collapsing onto her shoulder as she made contact with the ground. The grass sizzled beneath her, wilting and shriveling with every passing moment. She groaned, pushing herself up. In an instant, she was surrounded.

The crowd of six ruffians glared at her, sizing her up. She struggled to her feet, calculating her next move. She didn't want to hurt anyone. She only wanted to give James and some of the others a chance to escape. Titania had watched the van leave the grounds, so she knew at least Abigail and those with her were safe.

James appeared just behind one of the men surrounding her, who was holding a crude spear. He snuck through the chaos, closing in on her. Was James coming after her, the way these people were? Was he angry? Scared? Sad? Titania couldn't tell.

She didn't feel like she was strong enough to fight all of these people. She didn't want to. It had been so long since she had fully transformed; she had forgotten how much it took out of her. And now she was bigger. Older. She wasn't accustomed to using her wings, and now they had to lift even more mass than they had ten years ago.

The rioter with the spear lunged for Titania, and James seized the opportunity. He held his arm around the man's throat. The other rioters noticed and made a move to attack James, but James used the man as a meat shield to fend them off. Titania felt frozen, unsure of what to do.

As the man's weight began to sink from oxygen deprivation, James took the spear from his hand.

James let him go before he passed out. He pointed the spear at the circle, now down by one, as his victim was in no shape to fight.

"Let her go!" James yelled at the five still left.

One of them, a woman, sneered at him.

"And let the government take her back? Not a chance."

The woman grabbed for Titania, trying to wrap her arms around her. Her screams carried all the way to the compound as her skin melted on contact.

James used the opportunity to swipe the spear against the back of the knees of the enemy closest to him. The man cried out in pain as he pitched forward and fell to the ground. James made eye contact with her, then glanced at the woods, and Titania knew they had the same idea. They knew the woods like the back of their hands, thanks to Titania's insistence on sneaking around. She nodded and willed the heat to intensify in her feet.

The grass beneath her burned, fire spreading out around her in a circle. The rioters stepped back out of necessity and shock. The ring pushed them further and further away. Titania pivoted on a dime and ran, not even looking back to see if James was following her.

Footsteps carried behind her, and she hoped they were his. She went as far and as fast as her legs could carry her. Past the logs laying on the forest floor, the moss covering the wild oak trees, the fairy circles of mushrooms glowing with contamination, and past the point that they could see Lone Leaf any longer.

She heard the sounds that rang out from the compound in chaos. Their home for the past ten years was being brought down by contamination on the inside and rioters on the outside. By the end of the day, there would be nothing to go back to. A lump formed in her throat as she considered that it might as well have been on fire, just like her. Titania stole a glance backward, even though she knew she couldn't see it from here. James was there, watching her running ahead of him in wonderment.

Titania couldn't bear to meet his gaze. She kept running, leaving behind destructive footprints in her wake.

CHAPTER SEVEN

A piercing alarm reverberated through the lab.   Silen's hands flew to cover his ears. He snarled. Realization softened his face, giving way to giddy laughter.

Silen grasped at every drawer and cabinet, frantically throwing them open, trying to find the source of the sound. He couldn't remember where he had kept it. He had moved its hiding spot so many times to avoid accidental discovery or confiscation that he had lost track of where he was currently keeping it.

The drawers and cabinets came up empty. He wiped away beads of sweat that were gracing his forehead. He needed to find the blasted thing before someone came in.

If he could find it before that, he could pass the noise off as a smoke alarm he had set off. After a few more minutes of searching, he set a burner on and put a smaller piece of plastic on it to make his cover story more believable. The smell was putrid, but it helped him focus his mind.

"Ah!" he exclaimed as the location came to him.

Silen knelt and opened the cabinet below the sink. He slipped his hand in, feeling at the pipe. A wave of relief fell over him as he felt the tracker taped to the back of it. It was a good hiding space but, unfortunately, the acoustics below the sink were disorienting.

He clicked the volume down before ripping the tape off. He pulled the wad of tape and tracker out together. Silen grinned down at it, relishing all that this manically blinking little object represented.

He stood, smoothing out his lab coat with a satisfied smirk.

A guard burst in through the door. Silen had just enough time to pocket the device.

"What in tarnation is going on in here?" The guard asked.

He crinkled his nose at the smell of the burnt plastic.

Silen waved his hand in front of his face and forced himself to cough.

"Nothing to worry about," he purred. "I've gotten it taken care of."

The guard raised an eyebrow, looking Silen up and down. He surveyed the disheveled cabinetry and scattered items from Silen's disorganized workflow. "Looks to me like all you've taken care of is making this place a mess," the guard snorted.

"Science is often messy," Silen said with pride, having no care for the guard's opinions.

The guard rolled his eyes and closed the door, leaving Silen alone with his mayhem. They were used to his eccentricities by now. And, thankfully, it made them underestimate his capabilities.

"Finally." Silen pulled the tracker out and looked at the radar.

The signal was strong! And closer than he'd dared hope. If he left now, he should be able to find her.

He grabbed his coat and bag off of the counter and sped out the door.

The same guard stopped him as he tried to leave out of the side of the compound.

"Where do you think you're going?" the guard growled.

"Just out for some fresh air," Silen said earnestly. "To clear all the chemicals out of my lungs, you understand?"

The guard knew that nobody was to go out without clearance, but Silen hoped that this would be a convincing excuse.

"You could probably use that," the guard said sarcastically.

Silen bit down on the curses he wanted to hurl for the disrespect. He knew if he blew up, he'd lose any chance of getting outside.

"Just for a few minutes," the guard said. He opened the door. Silen felt his stomach do somersaults at the sight of freedom.

"Thank you," he groveled. "Thank you so much!"

The guard sneered. "Just go. Don't tell anyone I let you out."

"I won't," Silen said as he walked out of the door. "Don't worry." He took a quick look at the tracker and set out. By the time the guard realized he hadn't come back, he'd be well on his way to her: his greatest creation. Having her back would change everything.

Everyone would stop treating him like a crazed old man, locked away as a mad scientist whose life and career were over. People would respect him for the genius he was. He'd have the most powerful superhuman ever created.

He could hardly stand it! She wouldn't get away from him, not this time.

CHAPTER EIGHT

Titania could hear James panting. She worried about him; he sounded really rough—more than he should have. How long had they been running for? They'd gone through the entire forest near the compound and down a deserted road for at least five miles. Titania didn't like this land. It was so flat, you could see for a long way. They were so exposed.

She glanced to see if there were signs anyone had followed them. By this point, if anyone had been able to, they'd be able to see them. But when she looked back, she saw nothing. Not even her own burning footprints, which was a small consolation to ward off the anxiety of being tracked.

"There," Titania said.

She pointed to a small cluster of trees half a mile away.

James couldn't respond except to nod once. He was breathing so hard. She felt awful for him.

Titania felt her own resilience waning as they came up on the trees. The branches were almost bare; they twisted and contorted in unusual directions, but they would serve for some cover.

A tiny creek ran through the trees, and through a pipe under the road to the other side. It looked delightful to her burning body. James collapsed under the canopy of the branches and remaining auburn leaves. He rolled over to the water and dipped both hands in. He cupped them and brought some up to his face.

"No!" Titania warned him.

She knew there could be all sorts of contamination in the water. He looked at her, startled and delirious.

Titania cupped her hands and dipped them in. Steam curled up from the water as she superheated it with her skin. The first time she pulled up a handful, it evaporated instantly. She crinkled her nose in frustration.

She tried again. And again. And again.

Her frustration grew hotter than her skin. She could heat the water and then pour it into James' hands, but then it would burn him!

Titania searched around for a vessel they could use to hold the water so it could cool down. She took a fallen branch and wrapped her hands around two spots where she wanted it to break. Once she weakened it by charring through the wood, she put it over her knee and snapped it in both places.

She looked over at James, who seemed to be slipping out of consciousness. Titania rushed to burn a hole in the wood to make a cup. She dipped it into the water to rinse it out, filled it with water, set it down, and dipped her fingers in to heat the water for a few seconds.

She scooted it over to James. His eyelids fluttered open. He propped himself up on his side and took the cup.

"Blow on it, it's hot," Titania cautioned.

James weakly obeyed. After a few long minutes, Titania nodded. "Go ahead," she urged, hoping that the water had cooled enough not to burn him. James took a tentative sip, color returning to his face.

He began coughing violently. Titania moved to pat his back, but then remembered she couldn't without burning him. He held up a hand, letting her know it was okay.

James recovered his composure. He gave her a strained smile and held up the makeshift cup.

"Thank you," he said with a strained voice.

"You're welcome," Titania said.

James leaned forward and scooped up more water in the cup. He offered it to Titania, who sanitized it.

She sat down next to him, keeping far enough away that the heat she radiated would not cause him discomfort. She pulled her wings in and put her feet in the creek, closing her eyes and relishing the cool temperature on her burning skin. Steam rose gradually from the surface of the water, on its way to join the puffy white clouds passing over them. Titania welcomed the patches of shade they provided.

James looked her up and down.

Titania's cheeks burned under his scrutiny. More than they already did from her condition. From the moment Adrienne had grabbed her, she knew they would be having this conversation today.

The very conversation she had put off for years and years. This wasn't how she had wanted to tell him, as runaways in the wilderness. She wasn't ready. But here it was, staring her in the face all the same.

"So," James said, "Um—"

She cut him off with the wave of her hand.

"I should've told you sooner," Titania whispered. "I'm sorry."

He chewed on his lip.

"Are you…" He searched for an appropriate word. "Okay?"

Titania didn't meet his gaze. Instead, she stared at the creek and watched the reflection of the clouds on the surface. She found herself jealous of the water, with its beauty, life-giving energy, and calming effect. She was the opposite. She was disfigured, inherently destructive, and chaotic. She was a monster.

"Define 'okay'," she responded.

James unleashed a flurry of questions. "Are you in pain? What happened? How long has this been going on? What… are you?"

"In order," Titania turned to him as she spoke, "Yes, I am in pain. Everything is literally on fire—"

"How do we stop it?" James cut her off.

She could see how horrified he was. She just didn't know if it was at her, or for her.

Titania shook her head in frustration.

"I don't know! I've only ever done this once before," she explained.

"What do you mean?" James said, eyes wide.

"I've only ever had my whole body like this one other time," Titania muttered. "The first time."

"When was that?" James asked.

"You know how my mom left me at a compound when I was little, about ten years ago?" Titania said.

James got up and, for a moment, Titania thought it was to leave. He began pacing furiously.

"I remember. What about it?" he asked.

"There was a man there. I thought we were friends. He was so nice to me. He protected me and taught me so many things, but…" Titania shut her eyes. The pain was too much.

James cocked his head, waiting for her to go on.

"He did this to me. I thought we were working to save people. That's what he told me. It was my fault," she blubbered. "I said okay. But I didn't know! I didn't know."

Titania sobbed. The rivers of flame in her skin sparked, her cheeks sizzling from the moisture.

"You can't believe this is your fault," James said, balling his fists. "You were a child."

"It doesn't much matter now, does it?" Titania barked.

"Is this why you won't let me touch you?" James' voice cracked. "Is that what triggers it?"

Titania's heart wrenched. She nodded, meeting his crystal green eyes for a brief moment.

"I'm going to fix this," James vowed, his eyes wide. "I'm going to get you help."

Titania looked up at him through her tears. She didn't see how, but she also didn't see any point in arguing with someone in shock.

James leaned up against a tree to steady himself.

"Did anyone know before now?" he asked under his breath.

Titania couldn't tell if he was asking to see if she hadn't told him because she didn't trust him, or if he just wanted to know who they might be up against.

"The only person who knows is the man that... made me." Titania choked out the last two words.

"Look at me," James demanded. He knelt in front of her, reaching out to hold her hand before he remembered he couldn't. He shook himself to regain his focus.

"He did not make you. You are yours, regardless of what anyone has done to you." His voice was stern.

She couldn't keep eye contact with him, so she closed her eyes.

When she opened them again, she found him a few feet away, surveying the area. She saw him looking at the position of the sun and what lay in each direction. She knew they wouldn't be going back the way they came, but where else were they going to go?

It had been late morning when they discovered the rioters. Between the fighting and the running, it was creeping toward evening. They needed to find a place to stay for the night, and they didn't have much time to decide where to go.

"What are we going to do?" Titania asked.

"I think I have a plan, but it'll take three days to get where we need to go." James folded his arms. "And that's if we can get adequate food and water on the trip."

Titania hadn't even considered food. She probably wouldn't find herself hungry until this transformation wore off. But James would need to eat.

Panic overtook her. For the first time, she wondered if this transformation would be permanent. She only had experience keeping it from happening, not returning to normal after a full transformation. The first time she hadn't had to force it to wear off, it just did.

"What?" James read her face. "What is it? What's wrong?"

"What if I'm stuck like this?" Titania asked him. "I've never had to force it to go away. I don't know what to do!"

Her breath was shallow and rapid, she was practically hyperventilating. The sky felt like it was going to fall in on her. Instead of an endlessly welcoming expanse, it felt like she was being suffocated by it.

"Hey," James said softly, kneeling beside her. "It's going to be okay."

"You don't know that," she rasped.

"Just trust me on this one, Princess," he told her.

Though she tried to fight it, her lips betrayed her by curling into a half-smile.

One that James returned right back to her.

"For tonight," James said as he stood, "we need to find a place to sleep. Somewhere other than Lone Leaf, for obvious reasons."

He glanced back in the direction of their decade-long home, his face adopting a pensive look. Then he shook his head and offered a hand to her, but she didn't take it.

"Oh," James said, retracting it. "Right." He picked up a small blue pebble from the stream instead, fiddling with it as his cheeks reddened.

Titania gave him a consoling grimace as she lifted herself off the ground. Standing prompted a wave of heat to blast out from her, ruffling James's hair.

"Well, we are heading north," said James, taking the first step. "Maybe you'll cool down by the time we close in on the pole."

CHAPTER NINE

The sun was dipping below the horizon in a haze of red when James and Titania reached the edge of a town. They stepped lightly, unsure if it had occupants. But from the look of the dilapidated houses that lay before them on each side of the street, James didn't think so. The sign welcoming them to whatever this place was called had been vandalized beyond legibility.

James eyed the vines growing into broken windows as they passed by. The one stoplight in the town hung, bent at an odd angle with the glass shattered inside it.

It felt weird to be out in the open so far from Lone Leaf, he acknowledged to himself. Vulnerable, but also liberating.

Titania walked ahead of him, her head on a swivel. She moved a lot more swiftly than he did. His body ached from the assault earlier. After he had been kicked to the ground, his assailant had unleashed a torrent of blows upon him before James tripped the other man and scramble to his feet. He pictured the bruises that must have formed by now all over his torso. At least he had managed to protect his head.

Although, he mused, it pained him too. But he couldn't tell if it was from dehydration or trying to wrap his mind around Titania's state of being. She was, quite literally, on fire, and his brain refused to process that fact.

They didn't have enough light to explore the town in depth. James knew they didn't have much time to find a place to sleep.

He looked up and down the town square, scanning for any signs that someone had been there recently. There were no footprints besides their own, and no disturbed entryways. James wasn't surprised. This place didn't look like it had housed many valuables to begin with.

Even so, he didn't think they should stay in the town proper. Just in case.

Titania pointed down the main street. James followed her finger and saw a grocery store, just visible in the twilight.

"Look!" she said. "Do you think it has food?"

James frowned. Life outside the compound was going to be complicated. He didn't know how they were going to survive.

"Probably not," he explained. "I'm sure it's already been raided."

"Oh," Titania's voice dropped. "That makes sense."

"We can check tomorrow," James promised.

He smiled at her, trying to reassure her that things were going to be okay. He resisted the instinct to put his arm around her, not wanting to make her suffering worse, or add some to his own. James was already going back through his memory of all the times he had tried to be affectionate toward her, and she had rejected him. It relieved him to know that it hadn't been his fault, but the struggle to wrap his mind around the real reason was beyond his capacity to fathom.

James continued walking toward the other side of the town. He spotted a rusting barn in a field. The doors were open, so he could see inside. He squinted, searching for any vehicles or other items of interest, but came up empty.

"See that?" James pointed at the barn.

"Mhmm," Titania responded, still eyeing the grocery store in the fading light.

"I think we go there," James explained. "I don't know how many people might be in the area, but I don't anticipate anyone trying to find valuables in that."

They trekked across to the field as darkness fell. Titania's skin provided the faintest bit of light as it crackled, and the fire in her hair had dimmed past usefulness for seeing. The brittle hay stalks beneath her bare feet sizzled as they burned.

James noticed.

"Wait here." He urged her to come stand on the exposed dirt in the field, just outside the barn. The last thing they needed right now was to burn some place down. That would really put a target on their backs. The rioters weren't the only ones to have witnessed Titania's transformation, and even if they hadn't given chase, James had to wonder if any Lone Leaf officers would be motivated to pursue them.

He stepped gingerly over a rusted farming implement in front of the entrance. The light of the full moon filtered through the space between the boards of the wall, providing his now adjusted eyes with enough illumination to guide his movements.

James found a small welding workstation just inside on the left. He inspected the cabinet with the welder on top. The handles to the drawers were damaged, but they reluctantly creaked open for him. A pair of welding gloves sat, dirty and tattered, inside the drawer.

An idea struck him as he picked them up. But would it work?

He turned on his heel and spun around, stashing the gloves in his jeans pocket. James stepped over the rusted pieces of metal littering the floor on his way back to Titania. He didn't even know what some of them had originally been for, but he admittedly knew little about farming. He returned to the front of the barn where she stood, staring out into the night.

"All clear," said James. "And nothing's inside that's going to go boom. Come on in and let's see if we can get this closed up."

James tugged at the sliding barn door as Titania stepped over the threshold, but it wouldn't budge. It didn't so much as creak.

He frowned and pulled his sleeve over his hand to keep it from getting cut as he began trying to move some of the implements at the entrance to form a barricade. If someone tried to wander in during the middle of the night, he and Titania would surely hear it. And anyone attempting it wouldn't escape without a cut courtesy of the rusty metal.

"Will you give me a hand with this?" James mumbled, a little embarrassed that he couldn't manage the heavier pieces on his own.

Titania wordlessly joined her efforts to his, and the two easily moved the final few implements. James considered with a silent smirk that it was a good thing they were ruined with rust and disuse already. Now they had added slightly melted to their list of defects.

"Was it just me, or were you basically doing all the work to move those yourself?" James asked, eyebrow raised. "Are you... stronger now?"

Titania shrugged, not meeting his gaze. The fire in her cheeks glowed a little bit redder, and James wondered if that counted as a blush.

He surveyed the remainder of the floor, taking stock of the hay in the corner and the nuts and bolts scattered across the dirt.

Titania stood, nervously shifting her weight as she watched James gather up straw to make a bed.

He sensed her unease.

"It'll be okay," he assured her. "Nothing is going to get us here."

"It's not that," she said softly.

James turned his head to her. "What is it then?"

"I don't think I can sleep," she motioned to her burning skin. "I might catch something on fire."

"Not if we put you on just dirt," James reasoned. "I can push a bunch together for you to use as a pillow to make you more comfortable."   Titania wouldn't make eye contact with him.

"Hey," he said, closing the space between them. "What's the matter?"

"What if this doesn't go away?" Titania looked up at him with watering eyes. "What if I'm stuck like this?"

"I don't think you will be," James said truthfully. "But I do think you need sleep."

He knelt down and began forming a dirt pillow a couple of feet away from where he had made his own bed.

"I'll be right here," he patted his bed, "next to you all night. Nothing is going to happen to you or me."

Then he laughed. "Honestly, we are probably safer sleeping here tonight than we would be if you were still in that van. Or if we had stayed at the compound for that matter."

She walked to her bed and paced beside it.

"What's going to happen?" Titania asked. "To everyone at Lone Leaf? To us? To the world? How are we going to survive?"

Those were all good questions, ones that James had been mulling over himself. He didn't know what was possible, but he had some ideas.

He withdrew the gloves from his pocket, slipping them on as he made his way to her. They covered his hands up to the middle of his forearms.

"What's going to happen is that we are going to sleep tonight. Tomorrow we'll keep heading toward this abandoned compound I know of two days from here. I might be able to call an old friend for help if there are still transponders there. Those are the next steps. It is possible that we can both get fake clearance cards and new IDs and start over. If we go far enough away, nobody will know who we are."

That seemed to comfort her. Her shoulders relaxed. She smiled up at him through a sniffle.

"Thank you," she said, not making eye contact.

"You're welcome." He ran his gloved hand over her hair, gently stroking it.

She looked up at him in shock, grabbing at the glove.

"What is this?" Titania held his hand in place, bewildered.

"A fireproof glove." James grinned, waiting for it to sink in for her.

"May I?" He offered her a gloved hand to take.

She hesitantly gave him her hand, looking at him suspiciously.

He drew her in, putting a hand lightly around her waist, carefully avoiding touching her with anything not covered by the gloves. He could tell she was nervous by the way the sparks along her skin got brighter and hotter.

James hummed. It was a song they'd once heard when he had been given a contraband CD and player from a terminal patient. It only took a week before they had been caught with it and had it confiscated, but it had been wonderful while it lasted.

Titania's body relaxed in his arms as he swayed back and forth with her on the dirt floor. Her bare feet left small circular imprints as they went around and around. James could tell, even with the gloves, that there was a part of her that was holding back. But, for tonight, this was enough.

He could feel her getting sleepy. She yawned, a cute little yawn that made him smile.

He walked her to her makeshift bed and helped her down.

She laid her head on the pillow, not once complaining that it was dirt.

"Can we do that again soon?" Titania asked him.

"Every day," James winked as he held her hand. "Hopefully properly soon, too."

James ached to hold her close and never let her go. Truthfully, he didn't know how they were going to get out of this. He couldn't tell her that, though.

He laid down near her, listening as she tossed and turned. Her wings seemed to give her trouble. She couldn't lay comfortably on her back, even with them folded, nor on her sides as one was always squished. She tried lying flat on her stomach but, even then, James heard a small sigh of frustration escape her lips.

He cleared his throat and began singing her a lullaby as he stroked her hair. The beads of sweat that had formed in response to her heat trickled down his forehead. He was quiet, his voice a low rumble.

Titania seemed to settle in. His eyes grew heavy as he sang, and soon enough, he himself was fast asleep.

CHAPTER TEN

Titania laid completely still and listened to James sing. It was a rare occurrence; she cherished every second. It felt strange to be near him at this time of night. That wasn't something they had been afforded at the compound, with its strict curfews and segregated dorms.

He had an amazing voice, though she was too embarrassed to tell him so.

She felt a twinge of disappointment and guilt when his voice dropped off and he fell asleep. All that remained was the creaking sound in the rafters as the breeze blew through.

She laid there and listened to it for what seemed like hours.

Titania knew James had meant to lull her to sleep, but she had fought against it to hear him sing. And because she didn't trust that she wasn't going to burn the place down.

She rolled from her back to her side, looking out across the barricade they had made. The moonlight cast an eerie glow across the small field and unlit town. The longer she stared at it, the more unbelievable it seemed. Surely there was something or someone out there. Surely there was more to the world than the compounds and the desolation between them.

Titania wondered what had happened to everyone in this town. Had they died? Were the kids that lived there sold to a government compound like she had been? Had entire families given up their freedom for the 'greater good'?

Her stomach twisted. What did her own home look like now? She shuddered at the thought of her mom, passed out in the easy chair with a bottle in her hand, no longer breathing as the world crumbled. Titania took a deep, steadying breath.

She pushed herself up off the ground and stood. She tiptoed over to the barricade, careful not to wake James.

Titania approached the farm equipment to size up the best way to cross over it. She didn't want to tip any pieces and cause a ruckus. James didn't have the stamina she did to travel. He needed all the rest he could get before they headed back out.

Unlike him, she was superhuman.

Unlike him, she was a monster.

She looked down at her burning hands. Whatever that man had done to her, it helped in that respect. She was just now feeling fatigued after the events of the last day.

It made her sick to know that Silen would be proud of that fact.

Titania extended her wings out so they wouldn't get caught on anything and swung her leg over the rusted metal, hopping over to the other side.

"Ouch!" she said in surprise.

Her hands flew to her mouth. She hadn't meant to be that loud!

Titania spun around to see James turn over in his sleep. She held her breath as she waited for him to wake up. It was a minute or two before she felt confident that he would stay asleep. Her heart still beat wildly, but she had slowed it close to its normal pace.   She bent down to see what had caused her so much pain. There was a slit in the skin on the back of her calf.

Her normal, healthy skin. Despite the pain and blood, Titania felt relief. This was a sign that James had been right! She was going to be okay; this transformation wouldn't last forever.

Though it pained her, she pressed a finger along the cut to disinfect and cauterize the wound. She tried not to burn it too deeply in hopes it wouldn't scar. The smell of her flesh burning was nauseating, but it was by far better than dying of an infection.

She inspected the rest of her body but found that the only patch of completely normal skin was on the back of her right calf. It was spreading, though. She hoped it would be quick.

Titania tucked her wings back in and stepped along the bare ground with renewed vigor, soaking in the moonlight. She hadn't realized how good it would feel to be outside the compound. For as much uncertainty as there was, it was so freeing! She would never have to go back. She would never have to hide out like a rat in a cage in that dreadful place again. That wasn't even an option, because they would certainly lock her away to be experimented on and used.

Most of all, she didn't have to keep what she was away from James anymore.

She looked back at him, sleeping in the darkness on the floor of the barn. Titania wished she could be everything he deserved. She wished she hadn't destroyed his opportunity to go to Vandament. Sometimes she wondered if he pursued her because she was familiar. Even now, she wondered what he really thought about this. About her.

Something rustled behind her. She spun around and saw a small animal bobbing up and down among the stalks.

"Oh," she said to herself, "it's probably just a mouse."

A red fox got within five feet of her before they both noticed each other.

She screamed at the top of her lungs before realizing that she was more of a threat to it than it was to her.

It stood, poised to run. She matched it, knees bent and wings spread, ready to take flight. Its eyes bored into hers, stealing split-second glances at her body. Did this fox even remember what humans looked like? She supposed she didn't look human anyhow. She wasn't, really. As their eyes locked, for a moment she could have sworn she saw a flicker of concern. The fox crept closer, but then froze in place.

Its eyes widened. The fox darted off in the direction of the mouse that was surely long gone.   Titania exhaled the breath she had been holding. Being that close to a wild animal was exhilarating; she hadn't experienced it at all in the ten years she'd been at the compound.

She turned to go back to the barn and gasped.

James stood there, a crowbar in hand. She'd nearly run right into him. He rested the dark metal on his shoulder and rubbed his bloodshot eyes.

"What was that?" he croaked.

"A fox." Titania grimaced, clamping her wings down against her back. "I'm sorry I woke you up. I was just getting some fresh air when it startled me."

"That's okay." He yawned. "I don't think I could get back to sleep even if I wanted to. It wasn't super restful. How about we head out a little early?"

"Okay," Titania agreed, though she was certain he needed more rest than that.

She felt terrible about having woken him, but she knew she wouldn't be sleeping at all.

Titania followed James as he led her up to the road. The night air was quiet, such that you could hear even the faintest of noises. Titania's muscles stayed coiled as she took in every little sound and smell, from the soft rustling of leaves to the long-forgotten oil stench of a spill on the road. James looked back to check on her as they moved toward the main street of the town. The street looked so much different in the dark. It was spooky to be surrounded by so many lifeless, empty buildings.

James stepped up onto the sidewalk in front of the grocery store and offered Titania a hand up. She smiled and cleared her throat, showing off the rivers of fire in her hand.

"Thanks though," Titania told him.

She thought she saw a faint grimace, but she couldn't be sure. She knew this was a lot for him to take in, and it would probably take a while before he remembered that he really couldn't touch her without pulling the gloves out of his pockets.

Titania stepped up beside him and followed him toward the door. It was one of those automatic sliding doors that she had played with as a kid. It was stuck wide open, with no power left to operate it, and probably rusted out mechanisms besides. She poked her head inside. It was pitch black.

"How are we going to find anything?" she asked James.

"We won't," he asserted. "I promise you this place has been raided already." He stepped across the threshold and Titania followed.

Just inside, Titania looked up and saw cobwebs in the corners of the doorway. She reached out toward them, using the dim fiery light emanating from her hand to see them better, and the heat accidentally caused one to shrivel up.

"Sorry," she whispered to the spider, "I'm sorry, I'm sorry..."

She backed away from the web, almost bumping into James. He chuckled at her little mishap.

"What?" she demanded, cheeks flushing.

"Oh nothing," he winked. "Princess."

"I'm not a princess!" she protested.

"Maybe you're right," James conceded, "I don't actually know what kind of royalty talks to spiders..."

"You're... You're..." Titania sputtered.

"Irresistibly insufferable?" James peered down at her, arms folded over his chest.

Titania glared at him, fighting to keep a smile from twisting across her face.

"Hey!" Titania exclaimed.

She closed the space between them, staring up at him with indignation. She never won their little staring contests, but that didn't change the fact that she had to try.

Her face fell as she noticed the glow from her skin illuminating something shiny in his shirt pocket.

"Wait," she stared at the reflection of the fire. "What's that?"

James stared down at her with a smirk.

"What's what?" he asked.

She pointed to the reflective object in his pocket. "Oh," said James.

He patted his pocket and pulled up a cylinder-shaped object that Titania could barely make out.

"This?" he clarified. "This is just my penlight."

He clicked the top of it to show how it worked. A small circle of light illuminated the corner of the store he shone it on. It was covered in dust and cobwebs.

"It's for checking inside people's throats," James explained.

Titania raised an eyebrow at him. "You have a light and we're standing here in the dark?" "Sorry," he brushed the back of his neck and shrugged. "Didn't think of it."

"Well, let's check this place out and get out of here." Titania shivered. "It's giving me the creeps!"

They heard a sizzle when she picked her feet up and looked down. James shone the light where she had been standing. Her footprints had melted through part of the linoleum floor.

"We'll have to be quick," James said, shaking his head in disbelief. "Don't stand anywhere for too long."

He led the way, shining the penlight down the first aisle on the left.

Titania nodded, hopping from one foot to the other as she followed him.

Clear, upright freezers lined the wall. Titania walked up to one that looked like it had something inside, but when she gently pulled the door open, the handle melted. It was just as well, though. The stench of a dead rat laying on the shelf eye-level accosted her. She hurried to close it.

"Ugh!" She pinched her nose.

James shone the light down the row of barren shelving on the other side.

"Paper towels, toilet paper, tissues…" he read from the labels still stuck on the shelves.

"Those were probably the first things to go," Titania quipped.

"Probably. Easy to light a fire with." He winked at her. "Good thing we don't need help with that."

"Hey!" she pouted. Titania wasn't sure whether to be flattered or offended.

They rounded the corner and went down the next aisle. It was as empty as the previous one. James ran his finger over a shelf and inspected it.

"I don't think anyone has been in here for quite some time," he mused.

"I gathered." Titania eyed the molded leaves that had blown in.

The next aisles were comprised of two shelves that had toppled in on each other like dominos. Titania and James knelt, pressing their heads down to look beneath the crumpled mess. James shone the flashlight from one end to the other.

"There!" Titania pointed to some kind of canned items crushed under the weight of the shelves.

At least one can still looked intact.

James stood and tugged up on the top shelf, but it barely moved. Titania joined him, pushing it up with ease. She unfurled her wings and flew toward the ceiling, righting the shelf to its original position.

James moved to grab the can that they had freed.

"Bleck," James said with a gag. "It's canned ham."

"You don't like canned ham?" Titania asked as she landed.

He shook his head no.

"Man, that was a delicacy when I was little. If mom had that in the cabinet, I knew things were looking up," Titania reminisced.

Titania lifted the other shelf, but it was bent too much to stay upright. She motioned for James to collect the rest of the cans so she could place the shelf back on the ground.

"Who doesn't like canned ham?" she muttered as she returned the shelf to the floor.

Setting the shelf down caused a cloud of dust to form in the air. The smell was pungent. She tried to hold her breath, but it still managed to get in her nose and eyes.

Titania tensed, knowing a sneeze was inevitable. James watched as sparks flew from her face.

He stared at her for a moment and then began laughing uncontrollably. "What?" she demanded. "What's SO funny?"

"Does this mean," James tried to control himself, "That I get to call you a hothead?"

"James!" she shrieked.

She took a swipe at him, which he dodged only because she hadn't meant to actually hit him. If she hadn't been on fire, he wouldn't have been so lucky.

"Calm down, Princess," James raised his hands in surrender. "We don't want you incinerating the meat."

"I thought you didn't want it?" Titania teased.

James held up the three cans in his hands and shrugged, "I guess it is better than nothing."

CHAPTER ELEVEN

Silen's All-Terrain Contactless Vehicle glided swiftly above the stalks of hay in the field, miles away from where he had begun his journey. He had worried that detouring to get the vehicle would get him detained again, and he wasn't even sure if it would run after years in storage. But it had thankfully fired right up with the battery he had stolen from the guard's own ATCV.

Though he was making great time, the tracker's signal was fading. It seemed to be on a delay. Truthfully, Silen had expected to lose the signal by now. He wondered, given how long it had been going strong, if perhaps Titania was stuck in her transformation permanently. That was a known flaw in Generation Two. Still, he considered it better than Generation Three's propensity for being taken over by the animal minds. It made them fierce fighters, but they were only loyal to themselves and hard to control.

Though his ATCV was an older model, it was still relatively quiet, which would make it ideal for sneaking up on his prize when he found her.

He shut off the vehicle around the side of the barn and stepped out onto the stalks with a smirk, noting the charred footprints here and there as he walked.

She had been here. Perhaps she still was.

He tiptoed to the entrance. If she was inside, she would likely be hiding. And if she had seen him coming down the road, she likely suspected it was just any traveler, not specifically him.

Poor girl didn't even know she had a tracker in her blood.

Silen peered around the door of the barn. He frowned at the sight of the empty structure. He stepped over the conglomeration of farming implements that were strewn across the entrance. Had she done this? The melted handprints in the metal told him she had. His mind involuntarily flashed back to his escape from the compound she had set ablaze ten years ago.

He shook his head to clear it and returned his attention to the barrier. With her powers, why would she feel she needed something like this?

He spotted a makeshift bed of dirt toward the back of the barn, wing prints pressed into the dirt on either side of it.

"She mustn't have slept well," Silen mused out loud.

He looked up, a grin spreading across his face at the sight of the bed of hay.

"Oh," Silen's voice dripped with pleasure. "Had a slumber party, did we?"

Who could she be traveling with? Did she have a hostage that knew her secret?

Silen was eager to know the answer.

He climbed back over the mess of metal and hopped onto the ATCV. The tracker blinked a faint green toward the town, so he navigated in that direction. Perhaps he had just missed them in the barn?

The signal stopped just outside of a hole-in-the-wall grocery store on the main road of the town. Silen dismounted from his ATCV and crept to the entrance. He could see from the outside that the store was empty, but one of the aisle shelves was on the floor.

He tentatively stepped inside and noted the melted footprints.

"Not very careful, are we Titania?" he whispered.

He followed them along the path she had taken. Some footprints were very shallow, while others were deep into the linoleum. Finally, he stopped before the shelving on the floor. Silen crouched to see underneath, but it didn't appear she had been crushed by it. She had come into contact with it, though. Some of her feathers were sticking out from under the shelf.

Silen reached in, pulling one out.

He inspected it proudly, taking a moment to survey his handwork. His creation. She was lovely, in all her intricacies.

BEEP *BEEP* *BEEP*

Silen jumped at the sound of the tracker. He pulled it out of his pocket to see what the ruckus was about. His eyes bulged as he saw the now solid green dot on the screen. Something was causing her to go through the transformation again!

He had to hurry.

Silen fled out the front door and barely sat down before throwing the ATCV in drive and blasting down the road.

CHAPTER TWELVE

Titania's mouth watered as James cracked open their last container of canned ham. They sat under a tree on the outskirts of the city where James said their destination, the abandoned Oak Hollow compound, was.

Titania couldn't wait to get there. She had enjoyed spending the night outside for the novelty of it, but her hypervigilance didn't allow her much sleep without the safety of four solid walls around her.

James took half of the ham, speared on a stick, and passed the can to Titania.

"Thank you," she said politely as she took it and pulled a chunk out with her fingers. James nodded in acknowledgment.

Her stomach growled. Titania blanched. It was a good thing they weren't trying to be quiet. James let out a hearty laugh.

Titania flustered.

"You shush!" she told him.

But she couldn't look too angry with the grin she had plastered on her face.

Titania was on cloud nine. It seemed like things were finally turning around!

Her skin, her real skin, had been slowly coming back. She had both hands clear from the fire now, which made it a lot easier to eat. On the second day of travel, she had popped a piece in her mouth and accidentally burned her tongue from having set the meat on fire.

Being caught between human and monster was physically and emotionally taxing. She couldn't wait to be fully back to normal again. She was sure it would happen now, just a little slower than the first time she had fully transformed.

Titania never wanted to transform again.

She felt a twinge of sadness and anxiety as she considered what to do to avoid that. Would she and James never be able to be together? She had known his intentions for forever, and she felt the same. But this wasn't something she was confident could be fixed. How could she ask him to stick around when he couldn't touch her? The gloves could only help so much. What future could she offer him as a monster?

A pair of birds flew by them, catching her attention. They were chirping at each other as they played chase. They soared into the sky with ease, their colorful wings catching the sunlight.

Watching them made Titania a little sad that her wings were disappearing. They had been shrinking back into her shoulders a little at a time, and now they were almost gone. They were the only redeeming characteristic of her transformation, as far as she was concerned.

Titania and James watched the birds as they wound through the trees and into the blue sky. This area seemed so much more vibrant and full of life than the area around Lone Leaf. Not in the sickening sense that they had known, with the toxic yellows, neon glows, and twisted flora and fauna. It almost seemed healthy here.

She felt healthy here. The rivers of flame that ran through her skin had all fizzled out. The only things left to heal were the charred patches of skin that covered nearly all of her torso, along with scattered thumbnail-sized blotches on her arms and face. She hoped they could find some clothes at the compound they were going to before the patches all disappeared.

"Ready to go?" James asked. He stood up and wiped his hands on his jeans, looking patiently at her.

"Oh!" she exclaimed. She had gotten caught up in watching the birds and forgotten to finish her food.

She scarfed down the rest of her meat and stood up, ready to follow him.

They walked down a dirt path leading into the city. James wanted to avoid the main road, just to be safe.

"Do you think this Oak Hollow compound will have what you need there?" Titania asked for reassurance for the umpteenth time.

James smiled at her, hands shoved in his pockets as he walked.

"Yeah, I do," he answered. "And even if it doesn't, I can probably use bits and pieces to put together something to call out for help."

Titania nodded, satisfied with that answer. James was tenacious, she knew he would come through with this plan. They wouldn't have to wander, homeless, forever.

They stepped up from the dirt path and onto the first bits of concrete sidewalks in the city. Titania surveyed the buildings and shops that lined the streets. This place was a lot bigger than anything they had encountered on their journey so far.

"Which way?" Titania asked as the overwhelm set in.

James looked around with a somber expression.

"Give me a minute," he said. "It's been a long, long time since I've been out this way. Some things look a little different."

Titania sensed an edge to his voice, causing her anxiety to spike. Maybe it was because he was tired from all of the walking. Or maybe he hadn't had enough to eat, given their meager rations these past few days. She didn't want to interrupt his thoughts again, so she busied herself studying their surroundings.

Standing there, she noticed the grime that coated the outside of the buildings. Some were so bad that she couldn't tell what the original paint color had been, while others were just barely affected.

"I wonder why some of these buildings look practically untouched?" Titania wondered out loud before she could stop herself.

"Probably the type of paint," James explained. "Some of it has tiny little spikes built into it that prevent mold growth."

"Wow!" said Titania. She was sorely tempted to go up and touch it, to see if she could feel the spikes. "That's really cool!"

"Yeah, from what I heard about it, the idea for the technology came from the study of animals," James replied. "I think it was chameleon skin that works like that. Or maybe sharks."

Titania waited for James to go on. When a few moments passed without elaboration, she tore her gaze from the buildings and looked back at him. His brow was furrowed, and the somber look had returned to his face.

"Let's head this way," James pointed left. "If I'm right about where we are, we should find some landmarks I recognize pretty quickly through here."

"Okay," Titania said chipperly, trying to keep the mood light.

She followed close behind him, through the mold-covered buildings and rusted stairwells, the buckling streets, and cracked sidewalks.

"So when we were you last here?" Titania asked, interested to know about James' life outside of Lone Leaf. She really had only been to three places: her house, the compound with Silen, and the one where she met James.

"Oh, um," James fumbled, "I was around this area when I was younger. I had a buddy that I worked with at the compound we're going to. We were just kids, so I really wasn't working much. We got up to all sorts of trouble, especially since there weren't as many rules then."

"That's cool." Titania smiled.

After what seemed like close to a mile of walking, zigzagging through the town, James came to an abrupt stop. Titania nearly ran into him, she was following so closely behind. She looked up to see what he was staring at.

Ahead of them, a broken statue stood. It was looking over what appeared to have been a large body of water, one that was now reduced to a small pond. The statue was sliced down the middle, with the top half shattered in pieces on the ground below. Tiny waves lapped at a piece covered in moss. It looked like it had once been part of the statue's face.

Titania stepped forward, looking at James intently. He seemed frozen. Like his body was there, but his mind was somewhere else.

"Are you okay?" she asked quietly.

"Yeah." James shook his head in disbelief. "It did not look like this the last time I was here."

"I bet not," Titania agreed.

"We're getting close, though," said James. "We should be there in the next twenty minutes if we hurry. Then we can have a good amount of time to sweep the place and settle in for the night."

"Race you there?" said Titania, bouncing up and down in front of him in not-at-all restrained excitement.

James smiled at her antics, as she knew he would. She didn't like seeing him so serious. She was changing back to normal. Things were okay. It was all going to be okay.

They set off down the way past the desecrated statue.

Moments later, Titania felt the hair on the back of her neck stand on end.

She instantly began scanning the area. There was a park on the right side of the path and to the left a row of trees, which had engulfed the power lines above them years ago. She squinted, noticing a thin vertical line just slightly out of place from the rest of the colors in the trees.

"James," she whispered, still staring at it.

He didn't respond.

Titania turned to face him and found him struggling against a captor that had ambushed him from behind. The large man held a hand over James' mouth, the other arm tight around James' waist.

"Oh no," she muttered under her breath.

Three large, burly men took that as an invitation to advance.

"Get her!" the man holding James commanded.

Titania looked at them in horror, taking in their grizzled appearance. The one holding James had a huge scar jutting through his eyebrow, and he looked to be in his fifties. The other two appeared just slightly younger than him. One walked with a limp, while the other had the mangled remains of a right hand.

These two men rushed her, trying to pin her in. She moved to jump and unfurl her wings but was dismayed to find that they had fully disappeared. James watched in shock as the men took hold of each of her arms.

"What's wrong with your friend?" Titania overheard the man with the eyebrow scar ask James. "She get pushed into a fire or something?"

"She's ugly as sin!" the man to her right laughed.

The men had made a point to only grab her healthy skin, probably out of disgust for the charred parts.

Titania watched James struggle with renewed ferocity over the insult, and at the same time felt her own anger boiling over. She tugged her entire body away from her captors, trying desperately to wriggle out of their grasp.

They tightened their grip on her, sinking their fingers deep into her flesh. Titania raised her head and looked directly at James, who still thrashed wildly about to no avail. She tried to breathe, to calm herself. But she already felt the tingling in her veins and the tightening of her skin.

This was too soon. She had almost been free of her fiery prison. So close.

Something came over her as her body erupted into flames. She threw her head back as she cried out in pain.

The men shrieked as flames engulfed their hands, causing them to let go. They looked at each other in shock.

"AH!" the man with the deformed hand screamed in terror. "A monster!"

They stumbled backward and began running toward the trees. Titania's wings billowed out as she flew over them, chasing them away.

They entered the cover of the trees and then both let out a strangled bellow as they ran right into their own trap. The men dangled, suspended in the air by a camouflaged mesh net hung by a rope.

So that was what she'd spotted earlier.

"Titania!" James called out to her.

Titania spun around and flew toward him. She landed just in front of his captor.

"Not one step closer," the man with the eyebrow scar growled at her.

Titania froze. He held a knife near James' throat. She knew the implicit threat.

If she advanced on them, this man would kill James.

Her brain rushed forward with ideas, ways of thinking the situation through, but her body reacted on instinct.

Both hands moved with lightning speed. The man reacted as predicted, jerking the knife toward James' neck, but not before Titania seized both the knife and his wrist. She saw the small hairs on James' neck singe as her hand pushed the knife back, just shy of his skin. It gave way beneath her touch, melting against her palm. She smiled as she rendered it ineffective. A mess of slag.

She looked up to see the man trembling with fear and pain. He dared not scream, even as her hand burned through his sleeve and into his wrist.

A part of her relished that, just for a moment. This man had tried to hurt James, even going so far as to try to kill him! But she also felt a squeeze around her heart. One of pity and aversion to this. To being violent.

The man dropped his knife and released his grip on James. Titania let go of his hand and he took off, running back toward the statue near the water and abandoning his comrades in the netting.

"Let's get out of here," Titania said to a shell-shocked James.

He nodded, clutching his throat delicately.

CHAPTER THIRTEEN

James could not get the picture of Titania's transformation out of his mind. The anguish, grief, and frustration she felt etched itself into his mind's eye, as though he had stared at the sun and it had left a permanent visual tattoo. He wished he had been able to break free from the man that held him, to stop her from even having to rescue herself. Let alone him.

Just like that, all the progress she had made on changing back to normal had been undone. The guilt plagued him.

There was so much he didn't know about the outside world. Like Titania, James had lived most of his life in compounds. He barely knew more than she did about the way things worked in the wilds. He only knew what the government told them. He hadn't expected to encounter other humans like that on this route, most especially ones that didn't seem affiliated with any government agency.

He had thought he'd been mentally prepared for that slim possibility, but the ambush had come out of nowhere.

Those men had looked so rough, just like the kids in the woods at Lone Leaf. They really were fighting for their lives in the wilds.

How many others were out there doing just that? There must be more kids hiding out in the woods, and abandoned cities filled with people. They would need to approach the Oak Hollow compound carefully, just in case it too was inhabited.

He led Titania in a zigzag pattern toward the compound, using dirt paths and streams of water to obscure their trail whenever he could, just in case those goons ended up trying to follow them. Traveling with Titania was like bringing the sights, sounds, and smells of a campfire along in a mobile package. He thanked his lucky stars that she wasn't sending up smoke.

James hoped that when they arrived, Titania could get some rest. He wasn't sure how she would be able to sleep, but he knew she desperately needed to. Her body drooped from fatigue and her wings angled loosely toward the ground, as though she was too tired to hold them up anymore.

Clouds rolled in from the West as they traveled. Rain fell down on them, slowly at first before opening up into a downpour. James chuckled a little as Titania's skin hissed from the droplets of water. Her expression remained unchanged, brooding and solemn.

"It's going to be okay," James told her.

He knew she wouldn't be consoled, but he had to say it anyway.

Though it didn't put the fire completely out, Titania's skin seemed to calm down. The rivers of red dimmed, and the smoldering lessened.

"Achoo!" Titania sneezed.

This time, sparks didn't fly.

Titania faltered but caught herself. She moved slower, as though it hurt her to walk.

James frowned. "Are you okay?"

"Mmm hm," she assured him.

He wasn't so sure.

Even as they walked down the path under the canopy of overgrown trees, the rain pelted them strongly.

James walked behind Titania, surveying every direction for any signs of a threat. Oak Hollow emerged in the distance, just where he remembered it to be, sitting at the top of a small hill down the way.

"There!" James pointed it out.

Titania lifted her head lethargically to see what he was pointing at. She nodded without a word and kept walking. Something stirred in the pit of James' stomach. Anxiety kicked in. Something was wrong with her.

Besides the obvious, of course.

James tried to walk a little faster to encourage her to get there sooner, but she hardly noticed. Even when they arrived on the Oak Hollow grounds, Titania's expression and bearing remained unchanged.

The building itself was almost identical to the Lone Leaf compound. So much so that James would have almost believed himself to be back home, if not for the state of decay it was in. Somewhere in the recesses of his brain, he recalled being told that all of these compounds had been developed and built by the same company. Lumis, if he remembered right. They had clearly used the same style in multiple instances.

A tree lay on the roof of the compound, uprooted at the end. From the angle on the ground, James couldn't tell how bad the damage inside would be. Still, unless it had flooded, the building should suffice for a shelter.

"Stay here," James instructed Titania.

He jogged around the building, looking for any signs of recent entry. The fenced-in metal yard around the back half of the building was in ruins. The structure was still there, but the wire dome was misshapen and severely dented in random places. Weeds overgrew the yard.

James didn't see any obvious openings. Like the Lone Leaf facility, the windows had been closed and boarded. All were intact.

He returned to the front of the building. Titania sat in the driest portion of the walk, looking around at the trees. She seemed dazed.

James approached the front door and jiggled the handle. Locked! How were they going to get in?

Titania stood and lumbered up behind him, looking as though she may faint at any moment. James hoped that some sleep would set her straight.

He looked around, hopeful that there was a hidden key somewhere. He turned over a few rocks and the shattered remains of a light that had hung on the side of the building but came up empty.

James looked to Titania in hopes she would have a bobby pin he could pick the lock with, but anything that had been in her hair had long since melted away.

He heaved a sigh and began searching his pockets. There, in his left pocket—a paperclip! He used a lot of them for the medical files he worked with. That might work. He searched his other pockets and found a pair of tweezers.

These would have to do.

He had only picked a lock one time at Lone Leaf, and he wasn't exactly good at it. He'd only attempted it because he and his friends had their pack of cards confiscated to the office once.

James knelt and set to work, casting a worried glance here and there to check on Titania.

As he worked, rain soaked his dark hair and raced down his forehead. He occasionally brushed it aside so he could focus. He struggled against the lock, trying to get the right placement to trigger it to open. Titania quietly watched him as he worked.

After ten minutes of trying, James plopped onto the wet ground in frustration. The sun was close to setting and, at this rate, they'd be sleeping outside.

Titania knelt beside him and put her hands out, signaling for him to hand over the tools.

"Won't you melt them?" James asked, wiping away the rainwater from his face for the hundredth time.

"Only a little," she replied.

She reached out and touched a fallen leaf. It burned, but incredibly slowly. James guessed that was because it was wet from the rain, or else because she was. Maybe both.

"Okay," James said nervously. He set the paperclip and tweezers on the ground in front of her.

Titania took the tweezers by a single prong, covering it with her fingers. She bent it in and the other prong out, using the heat from her skin to make the metal more pliable.

James watched with curiosity as she took the tools and held them at separated angles inside the lock. She fidgeted them around a little, staring intently at the inside.

Click

"How?" James sputtered, swiping water from his eyes as if that would make it easier to believe them. "What did you do?"

Titania smiled weakly and handed him back the tools. They were hot, but not enough to burn him.

James turned the knob and pushed the door open. He motioned for Titania to step inside before entering himself and locking the door behind them.

They didn't need anyone else following them in.

CHAPTER FOURTEEN

James pulled out his penlight, clicking it on so they could see better.

Plants were growing through the cracks between the floor and the walls. James saw a red glow near the left wall. He took a step toward it to get a closer look. It was a functional punch-out panel! If that still worked, he should be able to find a transponder that did too!

Titania looked at the panel with wonder and reached out to touch it, but James put out an arm to block her.

"Don't," he cautioned. "If we touch it, it may send an activity notification out."

"Oh." Titania's eyes widened. She withdrew her hand, duly chastened.

James stepped through the entry room and into a hallway. The interior layout of this facility differed from the one they had called home for so long. It was much smaller, for one thing. Since it hadn't been responsible for any agricultural development efforts, they had allotted fewer funds to it. That meant that it would be easier to sweep so they could settle in for the night.

As they walked through the hallway, a door came up on their right. James opened it. A musty smell assaulted his nose. He exhaled sharply, trying to get rid of the burning sensation it caused in his sinuses. He swept his penlight around the room and found a puddle on the floor, reflecting light off of the surface. James stepped inside, thankful he had been wearing his work boots that last morning at Lone Leaf.

As he walked around it, James realized that the room was just like his medical office back at Lone Leaf. Except in this case everything was flipped around, appearing as the mirror image of the office in his memory. Like his, it was furnished with cabinets and a sink attached to the wall. The place where the exam table should have sat was empty, but the spot where it had been bolted to the floor was obvious.

A water drop landed on his arm, causing James to look up. The tree that had fallen on the roof had its branches dipping into the room. They blocked most of the rain from pelting through, but that didn't stop the water from running down them and onto the floor.

A desk chair sat just under them, the seat soaked with water.

James rummaged through the cabinets, trying to find anything that may have been left behind. Nearly all the drawers were empty, save for a few medical tools, like a stethoscope, a scalpel, and a rubber mallet.

Titania stepped into the room behind him. The glow of her feet went completely out when she stepped into the puddle that encompassed the floor. James took notice.

"Has water always helped with this?" He motioned up and down to her burnt body.

"Not usually," she admitted. "I think it's maybe because I'm really tired. Not a lot of energy to burn."

"Maybe so," James mused.

In the absence of anything helpful in the room, James headed for the door. He didn't want to sleep in water, but they might need to use this room since it would be beneficial to keep Titania from burning the place down. And it had ventilation for the heat to escape through the roof.

"Stay here," James instructed her before closing the door behind him. His heart dropped as he headed down the hall. She looked bad. While he had tried to project a positive, hopeful vibe during their time in the wilds, inside he was growing more concerned. He had not pressed Titania for answers about the man who had done this to her; initially he had thought that it didn't matter, what's done is done. But the more time went by, the more important it seemed, and the more he wondered about it.

Inside, he was also struggling to maintain his optimism that there was a solution to Titania's transformations. His medical training had never prepared him for this kind of phenomenon. It defied everything he knew about anatomy and physiology, not to mention his simple common sense. It was going to take a more scientific mind than his to unravel the puzzle of how to return Titania to normal, permanently.

James reached the far side of the compound and began working his way back toward Titania, checking every room for intruders as he went. He started in the dorm wing, looking under beds, inside closets, and even inside any cupboard that was big enough to hide someone. The building was different now, after years of abandonment. When he had walked these halls last, on the cusp of his sixth birthday, the place had been much nicer—not to mention much more alive.

He thought back to when he'd heard, a few years after leaving, about the building being decommissioned and abandoned. The government had started aggregating people in cities again. The compounds that dotted the landscape from coast to coast were to be retired, a few at a time. Facilities that had a scientific or technological purpose, in addition to a humanitarian one, would be the last to go. That was the only reason Lone Leaf had lasted as long as it did, thanks to its agricultural research.

Contented that the dorm wing was clear, James moved on to the commissary. He found it to be a damp mess, with water running down the walls, no doubt from holes in the ceiling that he couldn't detect from the floor. The dorms hadn't been much better in the dryness department. James considered whether the technology he had come to the building to salvage would still be operable, or if it would be a rusted mess. That's if all of the transponders, their only chance at calling for help, hadn't been taken when everyone here moved out.

No.

He couldn't think about that.

Tonight, all that mattered was making sure the building was empty. Until tomorrow morning, the question was open. And he could still hold on to hope.

When he entered the office of the Compound Superintendent, that thought of holding on to blissful ignorance was the only thing that kept him from trying to break down the metal door in the corner. If any transponders still existed in this compound, they would be down there, in the last-resort bunker for the senior officers of the facility.

Curiosity still had its way with him, and he reached out and tried the handle to the panic room.

Locked, of course.

James made a mental note to try this place first at daybreak. He contented himself that all of the doors to the outside had likewise been locked—he'd made sure of that. His thorough search had revealed a secure building with no way for anyone to get inside, and no signs that anyone had been here in a long while.

James sped back to Titania as though something was chasing him. This place was so creepy.

He found her almost asleep, a small chunk of her neck returning to normal texture and color. Her body lay half in and half out of the water on the floor. He closed the door behind him and locked it before kneeling beside her.

"I'm tired," she told him, her voice barely more than a whisper.

"Try and sleep," he said soothingly. "We're safe here. I checked, nobody else is here."

"I'm so tired," she said again, almost as though she was delirious.

James sat beside her where the water didn't reach and began humming a lullaby. He pulled out the pair of welding gloves and put them on. Cautiously, he reached out to stroke her hair. It wasn't on fire anymore, likely due to the effect of the water, but he could feel the warmth of it through the gloves nonetheless.

James hated needing the gloves. Hated not being able to touch her even when her skin was normal for fear of triggering the transformation. This pain of being separated, even when they were together, was more than he could bear. It was his own special kind of hell. He couldn't even imagine what it was like for her. All these years, he'd always thought that he was missing something. He'd never understood why she had become so icy at the turn of a dime anytime he tried to initiate physical contact.

Now he knew.

And he almost wished he didn't.

CHAPTER FIFTEEN

Titania stirred in her sleep.

The faint wisps of the darkest of dreams clung to the sides of her consciousness as she tossed and turned herself awake. There was this strange growling that made her nerves tingle. She swiped at the sensation in her sleepy state, but it wouldn't go away. Titania opened her eyes, disoriented by the feeling. Had she slept on something wrong and made a part of her back fall asleep?

A pair of yellow eyes stared her down. The faintest glimmer of a pair of teeth reflected through the dark. Titania's eyes widened as the creature inched toward her. She felt a drop of saliva from its mouth hit her leg and yelped.

James grabbed her arm from behind and pulled her toward him in an instant. His arm snaked around her waist, gripping her firmly. She hadn't even heard him before he latched onto her. Had he been awake before her? In her sleepy state, she almost forgot she couldn't just lean into him. His warmth and presence were such a welcome relief to having slept half in the water.

Her arm started burning where he was touching it, and she realized it must have reverted to normal while she slept. The creature's eyes dipped and Titania realized it intended to pounce.

James' penlight clicked on and shone into the darkness. The creature growled at the annoyance of having a light shone in its eyes.

Before them stood a large grey wolf. It was so big, Titania wondered if it was deformed. It looked crazed, its eyes wildly flitting between her and James. Titania saw the leaves stuck in its fur and realized it must have climbed the tree to get inside the compound. What kind of wolf would do that, she wondered? Did wolves usually climb like that? Titania decided she must still be half asleep because nothing was making sense.

"Ouch!" Titania gasped at James' tight grip.

"I'm so sorry," he whispered to her, briefly shining the light on her skin to survey the damage.

The fire spread out from his handprint as though her skin was nothing more than a delicate piece of paper in a wildfire.

The wolf yelped and took a step backward on its hind legs.

James and Titania looked up at it with confusion. Had it stepped on something? Was it scared of Titania? James moved her behind him in case the wolf tried to lunge.

Ever the gentlemen, he wasn't one to let her be closest to the danger.

The wolf took another step back and raised its front legs into the air. It was as if it was trying to stand like a human.

Titania rubbed her eyes from where she stood behind James. Was she still dreaming?

James shone his light on the creature. Titania sensed his muscles stiffening as they watched it. It writhed as though it was shedding off its skin. The wolf shrunk, its snout changing drastically. Titania's stomach gave a sharp twist as a human face emerged from the face of the animal.

"Stay back!" James commanded it. "Don't come near us!"

They couldn't exactly enforce the command, considering they didn't have weapons, but his voice was certainly convincing to Titania.

The last few changes overtook the animal. It no longer looked anything like it had before. There in front of them stood a girl, or what seemed like a girl. Her eyes were a mossy green, not the sickening yellow of the wolf. Her matted hair stuck to her head, large bunches hanging down in tangles. Most of it was dirty blonde, but there were patches that resembled the wolf she had been just a minute before. Streaks of grey highlighted it. She looked to be about Titania's age and stood on bare feet, haggard, with clothes torn.

"I," her voice faltered as she struggled to find it. "I'm not going to hurt you."

Titania and James stared at her in shock. She pulled something out of her pocket and James pushed Titania further behind him, causing her to call out in pain from the contact.

The girl held up her hands in surrender and placed a solar lamp in a dry patch on the floor, illuminating the whole room.

"Please don't hurt her," the girl begged.

Hurt her? Did the girl mean Titania?

"I'd ask you the same," James said curtly.

Titania stepped out from behind James, the wheels in her head turning rapidly. This girl had been a wolf just moments ago, and now she stood before them, fully human. How was that possible?

"Are you…" Titania began, looking down at her burning arm and holding it up, "Like me?"

"That is the question," the girl said solemnly. "Isn't it?"

CHAPTER SIXTEEN

James looked between the two girls, baffled.

The wolf girl saw his shock.

"Perhaps you should sit down," she suggested, pointing to the chair.

James nodded numbly. He walked over to it and plopped down, which squirted water everywhere. He was questioning his own sanity. He held onto his penlight as though it would save him from the overwhelming sense he had that he knew next to nothing about anything.

The girl looked at Titania with concern. "You're in bad shape."

James felt his blood boil. Was this girl blaming him? She was the one that ambushed them in the wee hours of the morning! He had just been trying to protect Titania. And it was dark! He couldn't have known he was grabbing healthy skin.

Titania looked at her skin and then back up at this stranger.

The wolf girl knelt in front of her, examining her with her eyes.

"I might be able to help you," she whispered.

Now she had James' attention.

"What do you mean?" he said, arms folded across his chest.

"I know a place we can go, a few days from here. Well, on two feet anyway," Luna explained, looking back and forth between them. "There is a doctor that can help… our kind."

She gave Titania a small smile.

"What do you mean, 'your kind'?" James said, his voice growing more heated.

He did not like this girl. Not one bit.

"Titans," the girl said patiently. "I mean Titans. Modifieds, Monsters… whatever you want to call us."

"Titania is human," James asserted.

Titania looked between them, hunching her shoulders anxiously as they spoke.

The strange wolf girl kept her mouth shut, not daring to go toe to toe with James. He could see her recalculating her tact. He didn't care if he seemed like a jerk. This girl was not taking Titania anywhere. It was probably a trap.

"Where are my manners?" the girl asked, standing and dusting herself off. "My name is Luna, I escaped a holding facility about a year ago now."

"Escaped?" Titania asked with intrigue. "How did you escape?"

Luna put a hand on the back of her neck and gave them a lopsided grin. "It's… kind of a long story."

"We've got time," James challenged her.

Luna gave him a wry smile. "I'm not on the government's side, if that's what you're worried about. It's kind of rare to have escaped, so I don't meet many Titans in the wild. How did you come to be on the outside?"

James looked at Titania, hoping she wouldn't answer. They didn't need to be giving this girl any information. They didn't know if they could trust her.

"It's also a long story," said Titania. "I've been out for a number of years, though. Well, for the first time. This time it's been a day or two."

James shifted, nervous that Titania was giving away information that could hurt them.

"Oh wow," said Luna. She thought for a moment. "So that would make you, what, Generation Two?"

Titania looked at her in confusion. "Um…"

"Generation Two?" James asked impatiently.

"Yeah," Luna said, as though it was obvious. "There are multiple generations. Generation One was the first of the Titan experiments."

"Titan… experiments?" asked Titania. The fiery crevices on her face paled to a yellow hue.

"Oh!" exclaimed Luna. "You… you don't know anything about this, do you?" She looked to James as if asking for his help.

James simply raised an eyebrow at her, bidding her to go on.

"Okay, well, starting from square one then." Luna took a deep breath and exhaled slowly. "The Titan Project began more than a decade ago. As I guess you can attest," she said with a nod to Titania. "The idea was simple: create super soldiers by infusing humans with animal DNA which they could access through epigenetic processes. It's a type of augmentation. Add an animal's speed, strength, stamina, or whatever to a person. Ugh, sorry," Luna sighed. "I feel like I'm explaining this really poorly. If my doctor friend was here he could—"

"Why would anyone want to do that?" James broke in, impatient. He wouldn't have believed a word of this if he hadn't seen Titania's transformation with his own eyes. It was too fantastic. But, then again, so was having a best friend on fire with wings. "Why would anyone want to do that to people?"

"That's the easy part, isn't it?" said Luna, cocking her head in that odd way she kept doing. "For power. To build an army. Probably also for the kicks and giggles of doing something no one's ever done before scientifically, if we're honest."

She lowered her voice and her face became deadly serious. "These are not nice people. These are not good people. If they were, maybe I'd have stayed with them."

Luna was quiet then, staring at the floor and chewing her lip. The look on her face told James she was mentally somewhere far away.

Titania was the first to break the silence.

"You said that I was… Generation Two? Does that mean they stopped experimenting with animals and moved to, like, elements or something?" She held up her right hand where flame guttered between patches of skin the color of charcoal.

Luna shook herself out of her reverie. "No. No, it's a DNA-based process, so it's been animals the whole time. The Generations are more… well, it gets complicated pretty quickly. I'm not even sure I understand it completely, but I can tell you that the different Generations were created within certain time frames."

"I'm Generation Three," Luna continued with a shrug, "which is the last we know of… But I've heard they've started experimenting on making a Generation Four. They are supposed to be the most powerful, and… well, we'll see."

"They're making more?" Titania's eyes darkened with worry.

"Oh yeah," Luna laughed. "Why wouldn't they? They have no incentive to stop! Like I said, an endless army of super soldiers is appealing to the government. It doesn't really matter who they hurt. But they'll get what's coming to them, I can promise you that."

"How's that?" asked James. His head swam with this new information, but he needed to understand it all if he was going to help Titania.

"We're not the only Titans to have escaped." Luna pointed between herself and Titania. "And we won't be the last. There are a whole lot of us, and we've been making plans to bust more out of the holding facilities."

"Wow!" Titania exclaimed. "How many more?"

"I don't know the exact numbers," Luna said sheepishly. "But I'm on my way to the safe haven where most of us are bunkered. You should come with me!"

"We'll have to think about it," James said quickly. Given the volume of information they had just learned, he expected to need about a hundred years, give or take.

"Of course." Luna smiled. "I'm sorry, I'm dumping all this on you right after I woke you up."

"It's okay," Titania assured her. "Considering what you've told us, I'm just glad we didn't get woken up by a government agent or something."

"That would suck. They have those tranquilizers and I—" Luna shivered. "I hate those things!"

Titania gave her a weak smile. "Are any others… like me?"

"What do you mean?" said Luna, cocking her head to the side.

"I mean…" Titania struggled to find the right words. She held up her arm to display the results of her transformation again. "Do any of them have this?"

James looked earnestly at Luna, curious about that answer as well.

Luna took a deep breath before speaking.

"I haven't seen anything quite like this," she said honestly. "But I have seen a lot of weird things. Splicing DNA is experimental, not an exact science. I know I have wolf DNA, but not everyone's is obvious just by looking. Like I said, I think the doc I know can help you. He has all sorts of tech to figure these things out."

Titania nodded before breaking into a coughing fit.

James' expression was tight as he rushed to her, knowing there was nothing he could really do.

"You need some more rest," advised Luna, an anxious expression on her face.

James watched Luna shift nervously from one foot to the other as he knelt beside Titania.

"Have you guys had enough to eat?" Luna asked, "Since you got out this time? I know food is kinda scarce."

James wanted to explode at her. Of course he had been making sure Titania was eating! He had gone hungry to make sure she got as much as she needed of the canned meat they'd had. But he told the truth.

"Probably not."

"Well," Luna suggested, "how about I go make myself useful? I'll hunt some food up for us and we can eat well when day breaks."

"Thank you." James studied her closely.

He didn't want to trust her. But, now that she was here, he knew better than to outright refuse help unique to Titania's condition.

Luna nodded at him. "You keep the solar lamp with you for now until I get back."

James watched as she climbed back up the tree and away into the dark night sky. An eery howl pierced the night after she disappeared from sight, sending shivers down his spine.

CHAPTER SEVENTEEN

The dawn's light broke through the leaves of the trees above them. Titania rolled over to find James sitting up in the chair, asleep, with the solar lantern perched on his knee. She looked around the room but found no signs of Luna's return.

Titania's head swam. She knew someone like her now, and they were outside of a cage. Just like her.

Could the doctor Luna had talked about really help her? Could they fix her so that she wouldn't get hurt every time James tried to touch her? Could they get rid of the animal DNA she had? Could she be fully human again?

James snorted, rubbing his eyes as he stirred from sleep.

He almost dropped the lamp and had to rely on his reflexes to catch it and put it on the cabinet next to him.

Titania was grateful for the temporary peace offering between Luna and James. She could tell James didn't like Luna, but she could hardly blame him. She wasn't sure what she thought of Luna herself. The possibility of knowing others like her was beyond what she could comprehend.

James looked at her through his thick, dark eyelashes. Titania had noticed through their journey that they always clumped together in the morning, making them even more impressive than usual.

"Did you sleep well?" he asked. His voice was deep and groggy.

"Uh-huh," Titania said, a genuine smile gracing her face. The first since she had transformed again the day before.

She still felt off, but it was less severe than it had been before. The sleeplessness had really seemed to take her down. Straddling the line between human and whatever beast she had been spliced with definitely took it out of her, too.

"We need to talk," James told her, going straight into business mode. "How about you follow me and we can check a room together for the transponders?"

"Sure," said Titania. She stood, feeling stiff from sleeping on the hard floor, partially submerged in a puddle.

James led her most of the way down the hallway before he spoke more.

"I think we need to be careful around Luna." James looked into Titania's eyes. "We don't know anything about her. I know she's like you, but it's better to be safe than sorry."

Titania nodded as she followed him. "I agree."

James dipped into a room and set the lamp in front of a large metal door. Titania leaned on the doorframe and watched as he pulled out the paperclip and tweezers and set to work on the lock.

"I'd still like to go see what she's talking about," Titania said, quietly inspecting her skin. "It could be my only chance to get the hang of this."

James set his jaw.

"One thing at a time," he told her. "Let's focus on getting the transponder right now. I'd bet every tin of canned ham we ever find for the rest of our lives that we'll find one down here."

"Not a confidence-inspiring bet for someone who doesn't appreciate deliciousness," Titania teased, sticking her tongue out at him.

He didn't answer. He was too focused on the lock.

Titania stayed quiet. She wanted him to be able to concentrate.

She knew he wanted her to get rid of this cursed DNA just as much as she did. But she also knew he didn't want to go along with Luna. And Luna had subtly seemed to only invite Titania. Titania was sure that if she pressed the issue, Luna would allow James along, too. It seemed Luna was heavily invested in her, and she didn't expect that Luna would give up on her over James coming with. And there was no way Titania would go without him.

She walked into the room, taking in what she could of it. The desk had a placard on it that read, "George Meeks,

Facility Superintendent." She had never been in the facility superintendent's office back at Lone Leaf — she wondered if there had been a metal door there as well.

There were some cobwebs in the corner in front of a piece of paper pinned to the wall. She reached out to disperse them and they collapsed in flames, melting away in an instant like cotton candy. The paper behind the webs was unreadable, having faded with time and water damage from the volatile climate in the unkempt building.

"Rrrgg!" came the sound of James' frustration from behind her.

She turned to find him with his forehead against the door, slumped in defeat.

"The mechanism is too big," he said through gritted teeth. "It bends the tools rather than turning."

"Do we need to look somewhere else?" asked Titania, moving back to join him.

James shook his head. "I walked this whole facility last night. Almost everything was taken when the inhabitants moved out."

"Maybe you'll see something you missed now that we have this brighter light," Titania offered.

James was silent. Contemplating.

Suddenly he turned and stared at Titania with excitement.

"You can open it!" he said.

"I don't think I'll be able to talk the tools out of bending in the lock," said Titania sadly. She held up her burning hands. "I tend to encourage things to bend."

"That's just it!" James stepped out of the way and beckoned her to stand near the door. "All you have to do is put your hands on the door. The hinges are on the inside, but I know where they are!"

Instantly, Titania realized what he wanted. Her heat had been dampened somewhat by the water she'd slept in, but both hands were still alight with fire. She hoped it would be enough.

"Okay," said James. "Put one hand here, and a foot there." He indicated a spot on the upper half of the door where it met with the doorframe and had her place her hand there. Then he pointed to another spot about three feet lower for her foot. "Now, take your other hand and put it here." James pointed to the latch between the handle and the doorframe.

Titania stood there, awkwardly balancing on one leg, for almost a minute.

"Okay, step back," said James, rubbing his hands in anticipation. As soon as Titania was clear, he gave the door a massive kick.

It didn't budge.

"Can you resume, if you don't mind?" James asked in embarrassment.

This time, Titania applied her heat for quite a bit longer. After a few minutes, she had to switch legs and put her other foot on the door to maintain her balance. James kept her at it until the metal on both sides glowed red-hot and began to drip.

Titania moved aside, and James gave it another huge kick.

Still nothing.

"Gah!" said James. "That one's gonna leave a bruise on my foot."

Titania gave him a pitying glance before moving back into place. As soon as she placed her first hand on the door, it fell backwards, landing with a deafening thud at the bottom of the stairs on the other side.

Titania and James just looked at each other for a moment until their ears stopped ringing. James was the first to break the silence.

"I loosened it for you!" he declared, pointing with a stern finger.

"I loosened it for *you*!" she shot back, utterly indignant.

They both burst into laughter. The sounds of their mirth echoed in and out of the room they had opened the way into.

It felt good to share that moment. Goodness knew they'd had precious little to laugh about since leaving Lone Leaf. The thoughts of what they had lost crept in, and Titania's laughter died. James noticed, and he cleared his throat while wiping his eyes.

"Well," he said, back in business mode. "Let's see if this was worth the effort."

CHAPTER EIGHTEEN

James stepped into the doorway and began descending the stairs, shining the solar lamp in front of him to illuminate the way. Titania followed at a distance of a few feet.

The room they entered was not large. Titania guessed that there may be room for eight or nine people to fit comfortably, before things became cramped. There were no furnishings except a single wooden chair in the corner, with a folded blanket draped across the back. A stack of three wooden crates sat next to it.

"At least that makes it simple," James muttered to her. "Either what we need is in one of these three boxes, or we came all this way for nothing."

He stepped over to the crates, footsteps echoing off the concrete walls of the bunker. James took the top box in his hands and lowered it to the floor.

"These look fairly flammable, so I'm hesitant to ask," he said as he examined the lid. "But the tops are nailed on. Do you think you could do something to open them without starting a fire in here?"

"I don't know," Titania admitted. "I'll do my best."

She walked over next to James and bent down over the first crate. There were quite a few nails holding the wooden lid to the rest of the box. She wasn't feeling her best, but her strength was still increased by her transformation — she could try ripping the lid free. She'd have to be fast though. Unlike the rest of the wood in this facility, these crates weren't in the least bit wet. They would catch fire in no time at all.

Titania stood over the crate and took a deep breath. In one quick motion, she grabbed the sides of the lid and yanked with all her enhanced strength.

The box came up with the lid, still held together by the nails. Titania set the entire thing down as fast as she could, but it was too late. The places where her hands had gripped the lid were already alight with flame. Titania backed away, knowing there was nothing she could do to put out a fire when most of her body was still burning itself. She looked to James for help.

James bounded over to the wooden chair and grabbed the blanket from it. He threw it over the box and patted it, stifling the flames. Miraculously, the blanket did not catch fire, and James successfully snuffed it out.

"On second thought," James panted. "Let's go ahead and do it the hard way."

Titania felt the heat rise in her face. Blushing while transformed was even more uncomfortable than normal.

For the next ten minutes, James worked the nails loose with his tweezers. Once he had one side of the lid done, he was able to wrench the remainder of the wood up and off of the crate.

"Let's see," he said as Titania moved cautiously over to crane her neck at what might be inside. James began unloading item after item of men's clothing. When he was done, he kicked the crate aside and grabbed for the next one.

James repeated the process and found several cases of bottled water inside. He took a grateful swig from one bottle before setting it aside to pour another into Titania's parched mouth.

Only one case was left. Sweat dripped from James' brow as he worked the nails loose. Titania wasn't certain if that was due to nervousness, or because of her. Sensing temperature was more difficult when transformed, but she had to assume she had raised the heat in this room by twenty degrees or more since they'd descended into it.

At last, James pulled the final lid free from its moorings. His eyes clenched shut as he did so. Titania understood — he didn't want to have his hopes dashed after all of that. But what she saw made her think that he needn't have worried.

"James?" she asked. "Do transponders have antennas and microphones?"

Titania watched as his eyes snapped open. His expression was one of disbelief.

"Yes!" he cried. "Yes!"

He lifted the device free from the crate it had shared with a few gas masks and several cases of bullets. Curiously, they didn't see a gun. She was glad this box was not the one to have caught on fire earlier.

"Titania, this is it!" James exulted. "I think it would work down here, but the signal will be stronger up top. Come on!"

He carried the square transponder, which was about as long as his forearm and half as wide, up the stairs. Titania bounded up behind him at a safe distance. She did not want this device to fall victim to any stray sparks. As dusty as this place was, she was liable to sneeze at any minute and never stop.

When she reached the top, James had already set the grey contraption on the desk. He flipped a switch on the side and a faint green light on the front of the device started pulsing slowly.

James turned a dial, flipping through the receiving channels and causing a broken static to appear here and there. It wasn't a strong signal. He turned the dial more frantically, searching, Titania presumed, for another human voice to come through.

James brought the solar lamp closer for better light, straining his eyes at the indicator to find a specific transmission channel.

"Cross your fingers," he whispered, and Titania didn't know if it was to her or himself.

He turned the dial back and forth in tighter and tighter arcs until he was satisfied. Then he opened a flap Titania hadn't even noticed, exposing a button terminal. He pressed a series of numbers and held the transmission button.

"This message is for Brandon Thelmes Unit 23," James cleared his throat, "James Belmont Unit 56. Requesting emergency assistance at abandoned Oak Hollow Post."

Titania held her breath as a thought occurred to her. What if this brought government officials from the Titan Project to them? What if James' friend wouldn't help them?

"James," she whispered to him after he took his thumb off the transmit button. "What if someone heard that message besides Brandon?"

"This is an encrypted channel." James tapped the receiver. "Brandon and I picked it a long time ago. It's really unlikely anyone else would try to use it, and even if they did, it would sound garbled to them. Brandon has the only transponder that naturally decodes the encryption and we are the only two people that know the code to use other transponders."

That made Titania feel a little better.

"What if he knows I'm with you and comes to take me back to the government?" Her anxiety was mounting quickly.

"Brandon is a good friend," James assured her. "He wouldn't do something like that. Besides," he added, "Brandon owes me a favor."

Titania raised an eyebrow, but didn't inquire further.

She watched James as he stared at the transponder. A minute passed. Then two. Then five. Then ten.

No response.

After fifteen minutes of waiting, James stood and paced. He squared his shoulders, and Titania knew he was trying to talk himself out of panic. If they couldn't get ahold of this guy, their only help would be Luna.

James pressed the transmitter button again.

"Brandon Thelmes Unit 23," he sighed, leaning up against the wall, "James Belmont Unit 56 Requesting emergency assistance at abandoned Oak Hollow Post."

Titania watched him, her heart breaking at his anguish. If she didn't have Luna's help to hope on, she would be in turmoil, too. She may yet be if Luna turned out to be a bad apple. Titania knew she trusted Luna a little too soon, but only because there was an implicit understanding of each other.

The crackling static of the transponder got louder. James straightened up. Titania walked over to him and watched over his shoulder.

She listened intently, trying to decipher anything that might be human speech.

James stood as still as a statue, as though that would make the signal clearer.

"Bran…" a voice came through the transponder. James shook with excitement.

"Unit 23… Post?"

"This reception is terrible!" James exclaimed.

He grabbed the transponder in both hands and rushed out of the office. Titania barely kept up as he ran to the back door of the compound. After a moment spent unlocking it, he threw the door open and bolted outside. Stepping out after him, Titania was greeted by an overgrown jungle of weeds and grass. James stepped on what was left of the walkway and held the transponder up into the sky.

"Brandon?" he shouted, pressing his finger to the transmitter, "Can you hear me?"

Brandon's voice mixed with the garbled static, "—there soon."

"Brandon?" James asked frantically. The transponder was making crackling noises.

James pulled it into the shade, cupping his hand over the green indicator light to see it better. The light pulsed in a long, slow blink before winking out. The speaker gave off an eerie shriek, then died an instant later.

Silence fell over them.

James manically pressed buttons, trying to get any kind of response. The transponder was dead. Titania could feel the hope slipping from him, replaced with a frenetic negative energy that now threatened to suffocate them.

In another instant, she was on the move again, following James as he raced back inside the compound and back to the office. He practically dove back into the bunker and emerged moments later carrying the crate where they had found the transponder. He tore through it using the light of the solar lamp, removing every one of its contents in the impossible search for another.

There was none.

James picked up the dead transponder and shook it. He listened and, hearing nothing, shook it again as he grabbed the solar lamp and staggered back out to the hallway. Finally, admitting defeat, he sank down to his knees. The solar lamp dropped from his grasp and bounced on the floor once, for its part never ceasing to shine.

James clenched the lifeless machine in his white-knuckled hands, and Titania saw his thoughts as if they were written across his face. They had been so close! If they had tried last night, would they have caught Brandon? Would the battery have held up longer so they could hear him?

"Maybe Luna has a transponder?" Titania suggested.

James rubbed his hand across his face. "I don't think that would be a good thing."

"Why not?" Titania frowned.

"If she does," James explained, "Best-case scenario, she probably doesn't know how to use it safely. Worst-case scenario… she has it because she is working for the government."

Titania's eyes widened.

Would Luna really do that? Would one of her own kind really work for people like the one who had done this to Titania, willingly? That was atrocious. Titania shook her head to rid it of that notion immediately.

"What choice do we have?" she asked softly.

James looked up at her, his eyes wearily searching hers.

"We're going to wait here for Brandon. I think he was saying he would be there soon," James said.

Titania frowned. What if waiting here meant missing her opportunity to go with Luna? How would Luna take that? What if she saw them as a liability if they didn't go with her?

James went rigid.

Titania turned to see a pair of yellow eyes staring them down in the hallway, the lamp's soft glow illuminating a rabbit hanging from the jaws of a large wolf.

CHAPTER NINETEEN

Stepping out into the sunlight again felt strange after having spent the night and most of the morning in what seemed like a cave. James squinted against it, his head pounding. How much of their conversation had Luna heard? Did her wolf ears give her super hearing? If any of it had bothered her, she certainly hadn't shown it as she padded down the hallway, whining for them to follow her.

Luna trotted out of the compound in front of him, happily carrying the rabbit in her mouth. He was thankful for the food, but seeing her carry it in her wolf mouth was disgusting. Did she have rabies? Would she know if she did? She dropped the rabbit on the concrete walkway in front of the building.

Titania stepped out to join them. Her gait was cumbersome, but her energy seemed to have improved. James took stock of her burns. He estimated a good 80% of her body was still completely covered.

James hoped Brandon could help them. Though he didn't want Titania to give up her opportunity to get help if they went with Luna to this doctor of hers. James suspected that no matter what, there wouldn't be anyone that knew what to do. He wished he knew about animals, but he suspected the combination of human and animal wasn't something he could learn to treat from a textbook either way. In fact, he strongly suspected anyone trying to treat these Titans, as Luna called them, was just experimenting further. But perhaps not? If Titania had been spliced almost a decade ago, perhaps there was some information and science on treating individuals modified with gene splicing. Would Brandon even know about the Titans?

James watched in horror as Luna transformed back to human. The transformation was even more gruesome in the daylight. Did it hurt Luna like it hurt Titania? If it did, she didn't show it.

As soon as Luna had fully transformed, James consulted her on what they should do with the raw rabbit. They had been lucky to have canned meat to avoid building a campfire thus far, and it wasn't as though they had needed one for warmth with Titania.

"Should we light a fire?" James asked Luna.

She smiled sheepishly. "I was wondering the same. I usually eat these things in wolf form, or if I absolutely must light a fire, I walk one way as a human to throw people off the trail. Then walk around as a wolf to obscure some of the tracks. It hasn't caused an issue so far."

"You've not encountered any humans?" James asked skeptically.

"Most don't live to tell the tale," Luna said.

"That so?" James crossed his arms.

"Okay," Luna admitted, "One lived to tell the tale. But they saw me as half-wolf and half-human. They ran away screaming 'Werewolf!' at the top of their lungs. I doubt very much that anyone they may have run back to would have believed them, and I certainly haven't been followed by them."

James exhaled a deep sigh.

"We haven't had to light a fire yet. Titania has heated up water here and there, but that was when her transformation was more robust. At this point, I don't think it would be good to have her try to cook it. But with the state Titania is in, I don't want her eating raw meat," James said in a hushed tone so that Titania wouldn't hear. "I'd rather not test fate."

"A wise decision," Luna affirmed.

Titania walked closer to them. "What's a wise decision?"

"We've going to light a fire to cook the rabbit," James told her. "A very, very small fire. I don't think those folks down the road will be paying us another visit after their encounter with you, but I still don't want to draw too much attention to ourselves."

"Folks down the road?" Luna asked, "I haven't seen other humans in this town."

"They were probably long gone by the time you got here," James explained. "Titania scared them pretty good."

"Oh." Luna smiled proudly at Titania. "That's good. I would be careful though, if the general public finds out about us, we'll have more trouble than just the government."

Titania nodded somberly.

James hadn't thought of that. Would those men go and tell others that they had seen them? Surely nobody from their home compound would have been able to successfully follow them out this far? They had been so careful to cover their tracks, or not make them at all in Titania's case. At least, as much as it was possible. But honestly, he suspected anyone who had seen Titania at the Lone Leaf compound would've been written off as a crazy person, and he didn't think she was very recognizable in her crispy lava form, anyway.

"Welp," James said, stifling his mounting anxiety, "This rabbit isn't gonna skin itself! Be right back."

He ran back to the exam room where they had spent the night and pulled the scalpel he'd found from the drawer. Upon returning outside, he groaned. The rabbit was so small! Skinning this thing would take forever.

The blood and gore didn't bother him, but he knew it would bother Titania. Especially gutting it. He was grateful when Luna began chatting incessantly to her and dragging her along to get some dry kindling. It took her attention off watching him prepare their dinner. It was a gruesome, meticulous process, but he had finished by the time the girls returned.

"And this one guy I was in with, he could turn into a snake! Creepy, right? But after a while… well, he lost his mind and…"

James loudly cleared his throat. He did not want Luna putting new fears into Titania's head, and whatever it was they were talking about sounded like a nightmare.

Luna cocked her head at James, a quizzical expression on her face. He drew his hand across his throat, indicating for her to stop with that line of conversation. Luna gave a quick nod, then looked back at Titania as she continued to babble on.

James was glad that Titania and Luna could relate. It seemed to be doing Titania at least a bit of good.

The girls dropped their kindling on the sidewalk. Then they arranged the lightest bit of straw at the bottom, some sticks in the middle, and two logs crisscrossed on top. Titania stuck her hand beneath the kindling, and within seconds, it was smoldering.

James snuck one of the smaller sticks out of the fire and pierced the rabbit's flesh with it. He waited until they established the flames on the logs before holding the rabbit above them. James rotated it carefully, making sure to cook it evenly. He didn't want Titania ingesting any raw meat, even if he questioned for a moment whether her insides were on fire as well. The color had come back to the normal parts of her face, but he didn't know how long that would last. Her system seemed to recover slower and slower with each insult.

"This smells so good!" Luna exclaimed.

"It really does." Titania smiled proudly at James.

He beamed back at Titania. "Thank you!"

Since he didn't have plates, the girls cupped their hands and waited for James to pull off pieces of meat and dole them out.

"Ouch!" Luna bounced the pieces in her hand. "That's hot!"

"Sorry," James winced. "I'm used to that not being an issue by this point."

"Hey now!" Titania laughed, already having ingested half of what he had given her without waiting for it to cool down.

James took a bite. It wasn't bad but, he had to admit, the canned meat was a gourmet meal in comparison.

Luna chewed on her portion hungrily, mouth open. James suspected her time fending for herself alone as a wolf had dampened whatever table manners she had originally possessed.

She froze.

"Do you smell that?" she whispered to Titania and James.

"Smell what?" James asked, not bothering to match her volume.

Something whizzed past Titania's ear and plunged into the dirt inches away from her.

"What was that?" She looked back in confusion.

James was already on his feet, positioning himself between Titania and the direction that the flying object had come from.

Luna took one look at it and whispered, "Tranq."

"What?" Titania asked, looking over at her.

But Luna was already on all fours, bounding away from the camp before the words left Titania's mouth.

James spotted the source of the dart at the edge of the clearing. A man stood in a lab coat, a wry expression on his face. He held the offending weapon in his hand, bringing it up to aim again. How had this guy found them? He didn't look like a ruffian. Had Luna actually been working with the government? Had she led him right to them?

"We have to get out of here!" James bellowed.

Titania scrambled to her feet with the grace of a newborn deer.

"What about Luna?" Titania asked.

"She's gone," James motioned to where Luna had run. "We have no loyalty to her, and clearly she has none to us. We need to take care of ourselves now!"

Titania looked ahead, flinching out of the way of another dart. The man firing them began walking steadily toward them.

Titania squinted, then set her jaw.

"I need you to touch me," she told James, motioning for him to follow.

"What?" he asked incredulously.

"Touch me!" she screamed as the man with the tranquilizer gun started running.

James looked bewildered. He did as she asked, though he didn't think it was exactly what she had in mind. He scooped her up in his arms, fireman carrying her toward the woods behind the compound.

Her skin was ablaze. It burned him, but he didn't dare let go. If he put her down, he was sure he'd never see her again.

Another dart whizzed by them, landing with an ominous thud in the bark of a tree.

Titania sat up. She leapt from his arms and toward the other side of the trees, her wings unfurling in all their splendor as she completed her transformation yet again.

"What are you doing?" James demanded.

He could make out only a few words between sobs.

"He wants me," she yelled.

Her bare feet burned a path right to her.

James tried to divert toward her, but she glanced back and chided him.

"No!" she screamed. "Just trust me!"

He watched her disappear into the woods. He knew there was no arguing with her. Even in her fragile state, he pitied the fool that would try to pick a fight with her.

James dutifully dipped into the other side of the woods, getting a few feet in before he felt a sharp pain in his ankle.

"What the—" he exclaimed. Had he been bitten by something?

He tried to look back, but the forest tilted to the right. Then it violently spun around and around. He felt as though he may throw up the rabbit he just ate, and he desperately wanted to never taste that thing again.

James heard a garbled voice as he collapsed onto a fallen log to steady himself. A tiny pinch pricked his ankle as the world faded to black.

Titania ran, her vision blurring more with every step she took. She burst through the trees and into a small clearing.

Had she been this way already? The world felt like it was tilting as she examined the ground. She didn't see any charred footprints in the clearing. But she couldn't be sure.

The forest was blending together. Her muscles ached from the exertion. The burning in her lungs made her dizzy. She leaned back against a tree, spreading her wings out of the way so she wouldn't crush them. The relief was palpable.

Her breath caught up in ragged inhales. She didn't hear anyone coming after her. How long had she been running for? She hoped it had been enough to allow James to get away. She hoped he was safe.

She sank down against the trunk of the tree and stared unblinkingly ahead. She was more exhausted than she thought. Every transformation seemed to make her more sick.

Titania sat at the base of a tree, unable to move. She knew she should get up, but she couldn't muster the energy. Fear paralyzed her as she replayed the scene in her mind. It had been a close call. What if one of them had gotten hit by those darts? She shivered at the thought.

A surge of adrenaline coursed through her veins, feeding the burning rivers. They took hold of her arms again. She knew who was after them. She recognized him.

Silen.

How had he found her after all these years? Had someone at Lone Leaf somehow contacted him? How had he tracked them? What did he intend to do with her? Drag her back and experiment on her some more? Torture her again?

The worst he could do was kill her. And, at this point, she dared him to try.

Her anger boiled over, steam coming out of her nose as she exhaled violently. Titania rose and paced the forest floor, the clover shriveling beneath her. She hated this. She hated that he had made her this way.

The thought crossed her mind to hunt him down. He had those darts, but she could burn him to a crisp so long as she could avoid being hit. Then he'd never do this to anyone else.

She'd never have to deal with him crossing her path again.

A twig cracked. Titania spun, every muscle tensed to fight. A large wolf stood a few feet away, its eyes boring into hers.

"Luna?" Titania whispered, not faltering from her stance.

The wolf gave a low whine. Its feet and snout began morphing into something unrecognizable as human or animal. Titania grimaced in sympathy for how painful she expected this was for Luna.

In her human form, Luna panted heavily, her tongue still slightly elongated.

"Why did you run off on us like that?" Titania demanded. Now that James wasn't with her, she had no trouble being the skeptical one.

Luna winced.

"If you'd ever been hit by one of those darts, you'd understand," Luna assured her.

Titania opened her mouth to protest, but Luna cut her off.

"Listen, we can fight later," Luna said. "That dude snatched your boyfriend."

It took Titania a moment to process this information.

"W-what?" she stammered.

"You know, that guy?" Luna said. "The one in the lab coat? Yeah, he snatched your boyfriend. Got him with a tranq."

"How do you know?" Titania narrowed her eyes. This didn't make any sense. James didn't show any signs of being modified. It didn't make sense for Silen to go after him instead of Luna or Titania.

"I retraced their steps. That Tranq fluid is smelly. There was a little bit of it and blood at the edges of the forest," Luna explained. "I sniffed out the trail and they were definitely going the same direction after that."

Titania's eyes widened. There was no telling what Silen was up to.

"We have to go after them! I don't know what Silen wants, but we can't leave James to fend for himself," Titania said.

Luna looked confused.

"Silen?" she asked. "Do you know that guy?"

Titania paused.

"He's..." She struggled to find a good way to explain it, "He did this to me."

Titania held up her burning arms and gestured to the charred skin covering her body.

"Oh," Luna said, her expression dark. "I understand."

Titania said nothing. She had a hard time believing Luna understood.

"This is the first time I've seen him since... since it happened," Titania admitted.

Chills overcame Titania. She faltered. Luna gestured for her to sit, concern twisting her face.

"I'm so sorry," Luna said. "You must be in shock. I'd be if I were in your shoes."

Titania's skin flared, vast patches of furious red fire burned across its surface. She shivered as though she was sitting on ice, even as the flames raged on. The edges of her vision started going dark.

"We have to go get James," Titania insisted. "I can't let Silen hurt him."

"Okay." Luna held out her hands and spoke soothingly. "I need you to calm down. You aren't looking so good."

"We need to go now," Titania pleaded, pressing the heel of her hand to her head. She reached out to steady herself, but missed the tree she had been trying to touch. She hit the ground with a thud, out cold.

CHAPTER TWENTY-ONE

Luna shook her head, her paws pressing lightly into the dirt of the clearing as she returned. She'd followed Titania's boyfriend as far as she could. She was pretty sure she knew exactly where his captor was headed, but Titania was in no shape to follow.

As soon as she came to, Luna was going to insist on taking her to Adam. If anyone could help this girl, it would be him.

Luna transformed back into a human. She took a stick and gently nudged Titania, which set the tip of the wood ablaze.

"James," Titania muttered. "Need to get to James."

"Wake up," Luna told her. "I need you to wake up for me."

Titania bolted upright, sucking in air.

"We have to go!" Titania insisted, carrying on as though she had never lost consciousness.

"You're in no shape to go after him," Luna argued. "I followed their trail a bit after you collapsed and I know where they are going, but first we need to get you to the doc."

Titania stood up, defiantly setting off in the opposite direction of the way Silen had taken James.

"That's the wrong way," Luna said dryly.

Titania held her head, spinning around and stomping forward.

Luna stood in front of her, blocking her path.

"Look," Luna said, "You're in no shape for this."

Titania frowned at her, frustration clear.

"We need to help him!" she insisted.

"Can I ask you something?" Luna said.

"What?" Titania asked, perturbed.

Luna chewed on her lower lip as she surveyed Titania's skin.

"What did they use to activate the DNA merger for you? Do you know?"

"I only had one injection when I was really little," Titania said impatiently.

She didn't like to think about it. She could still feel the sterility of the office, the cold shackles on her wrists, hear Silen telling her they were just for her protection, in case she had an adverse reaction. He was a liar. She knew that now.

"I see," Luna nodded.

"You see what?" said Titania, an edge creeping into her voice.

"Nowadays, they have an activation injection to encourage the merger of the animal DNA to your human DNA. But before that…" Luna's voice got quieter, "they used… whatever means necessary."

"You mean torture," Titania spat.

"I'm sorry," Luna told her sincerely. "It's unconscionable what they did."

Resentment flowed through Titania. Had Luna gotten a simple activation injection rather than being tortured? Was it really as simple as an injection the whole time?

"At first," Luna explained, "they thought that simply injecting the DNA would be enough. Their processes have always been littered with reprehensible evils for the sake of the 'greater good', as they say."

Titania buried her head in her hands. If she could go back and run, she would. Every fiber of her being begged her to, but she knew it was useless. It was already done.

Luna shifted her weight nervously. "This might be why you can't control your transformations. If we go to the cave hideout, they should be able to help you. It's a couple days away, but they are far better equipped to help you than I am."

"We can do that," Titania said, "after we rescue James. We're closer to him now than we are to the hideout."

"Right," Luna said. "But you can't control your transformations and they seem to be buggy. If we go, they could patch you right up and you could be at full capacity to fight Silen."

Titania looked down at her charred skin, continents of black between rivers of lava. She willed the transformation to recede. To return to healthy skin and prove to Luna that she had some control.

But it didn't budge. Maybe Luna was right.

"What if this Silen guy has backup?" Luna reasoned. "We could bring reinforcements from the hideout with us. But I don't think we'd be able to take on too many people by ourselves. Especially not with you in this condition, you literally passed out earlier!"

Titania knew she was right. But she wanted to scream. She wanted to cry. She wanted to take back having sent James in the other direction. She should've stayed with him. She could've fought Silen.

If going to this hideout meant that she would have a better chance of rescuing James, then she owed it to him. To make up for her mistake. To make sure that she would never have to be separated from him again. She'd be in control.

Titania nodded, acquiescing. "Let's go."

CHAPTER TWENTY-TWO

Silen burst through the door of the Whitetail compound. The boy laid across his ATCV outside, unconscious.

"Excuse me."

A young man of low rank approached him, trying to cut him off from entry. "You don't have clearance to be here."

Silen spoke slowly and clearly, "I don't need clearance."

A few older officers ran up behind the low rank officer.

"I'm so sorry, Sir," Anthony spoke. "He's new. It is good to see you in good health. Please come in."

One of the men took aside the low rank officer and spoke to him in hushed tones. Silen took great pleasure in seeing the boy's eyes widen and the inaudible whispers spread through the facility. It was nice to be somewhere he was appreciated.

"Young man," Silen called to one of the senior officers, a man in his twenties who Silen had never met. "Please escort my cargo to the medical bay."

Silen motioned to the limp boy.

The officer went hastily to the vehicle and plucked the boy up, his head bobbing. Cargo in tow, he followed Silen down the hallway to the medical bay.

It was utterly satisfying to flip the light switch on to find a pristine room with a few cages and restraints already waiting for him.

The officer placed the boy on the table and stood, awaiting new orders. It was quaint. Silen wished that he could have spent the last several years here, a respected scientist rather than just short of a prisoner. The freedom was immensely overdue.

"That'll be all," Silen dismissed the officer.

He was ready to begin.

Silen used the table restraints on the boy's arms and legs. He had used a Titan's dose of tranquilizer, not a mere human's. If the boy woke up on his own in any condition to fight, Silen would be shocked. But he'd learned to never underestimate anyone. Titania had taught him that when she was just a small child.

Silen pulled out a bottle from his bag and opened it by the boy's head.

The boy struggled away from it instantly. He coughed violently before opening his eyes and looking straight up at Silen.

A wry smile tugged at the corner of Silen's lip. The boy looked absolutely terrified. He loved it.

"Where is she?" the boy demanded. "What did you do to Titania?"

"I didn't do anything to her," Silen said with feigned innocence. "Not recently."

The boy raged against the restraints, his bloodlust apparent. Silen smiled. He liked to see a subject with good energy and a fighting spirit.

Silen placed his vials on the table, picking through them. He couldn't decide what he wanted to do.

He picked up a bottle with a green label and one with a purple label, settling on both of them. Why should he choose one or the other? He made the rules here.

Silen popped the cap off of two clean needles and pushed one into the first vial, stealing away its contents.

"So," Silen looked over at the brooding boy. "Did she tell you?"

"Tell me what?" the boy said through gritted teeth.

"That she wasn't human," Silen said simply.

"She is," the boy growled. "She is human."

Silen smiled, flicking away the excess liquid beading at the top of the sharp point.

"She's not," he said.

The boy followed him with his eyes, watching in horror as Silen approached him. The boy struggled, red scrapes forming on his wrists.

"And now," Silen said, forcing the first needle into the boy's flesh, "neither are you."

He grinned as the boy's screams echoed through the compound.

CHAPTER TWENTY-THREE

Luna trudged ahead in wolf form, scouting out the last leg of their journey to the cave. It had been a long two days since they had set out, and Luna was still in fighting condition. Titania was a different story.

Luna looked back to check on her. She'd left her to rest against a tree down the hill. Luna clenched her jaw. Titania seemed to get sicker and sicker. Half of her body was healed, and the other half raged like a volcano. Luna couldn't understand it. Even in the beginning, she had never had such trouble controlling her transformations. Luna didn't know of anyone else that did either, at least not that had fully turned back to human afterward. She also didn't know any Titans whose skin burned like that. What animal even did that? She couldn't think of any.

Titania looked like she would pass out at any moment for the last eight hours. And all she did was talk about the human boy. It drove Luna nuts!

Luna ran forward across the grassy hill and scanned the area, saying a silent prayer that she could get this girl to Adam before it was too late. She was in over her head with this one.

The grass beneath her paws felt softer than anything she had felt on their journey. The same glowing purple mushrooms she'd so often seen along the way lined the edge of the trees. She didn't dare touch them. Radioactive food didn't seem the least bit appetizing, despite her growing hunger. Her ears perked back at the sound of the birds chirping up in the trees. She could snatch one if only she could reach.

BLECH. Her human brain overrode the wolf side. Right. She didn't want to eat a bird, feathers and all. That sounded gross.

Focus, she told herself.

From the looks of it, Luna suspected it would take them the rest of the day to get to the cave.

She turned back, running to meet Titania back at the tree.

Luna started her transformation. It always felt a little funny, shedding the fur that kept her so warm. She didn't miss the mangy smell though; it always relieved her to get rid of it. Changing her snout was the hardest. It made her feel like she had to sneeze and that she had snorted soda on accident. Unpleasant, but not unbearable.

"You ready?" she asked Titania as her claws thinned out into nails.

The girl stared off into space. She turned her head slowly and nodded once. Titania tried to push herself up, but faltered. She fell back down, hitting the ground hard.

Luna winced and put her hand out. Titania looked at it for a moment before shaking her head and hoisting herself up. For a moment, Luna was offended. But then she realized that Titania probably didn't want to take the risk of burning her, even though both hands were now normal skin. Luna appreciated that.

As Titania stood, staggering slightly, Luna wondered if this was shock from what her body was going through. Or maybe shock from being separated from her boyfriend. Or something else entirely.

Whatever it was, Luna didn't like it. She didn't know how she was going to get Titania to the cave in this condition.

"Let's go," Luna urged her.

The girl fell in step beside her.

"I'm so tired," Titania said. Then her face fell. "I'm sorry, I didn't mean to complain."

"It's okay," Luna looked at her incredulously. This girl was a little weird. Of course she was tired! They'd been walking for two days with her in half transformation. Did she really think Luna would hold it against her that she was tired?

As they started walking up the hill, Titania faltered. Luna took a hold of her side and tried to prop her up without getting burned. Once they were at the top, Luna let go. Sweat beaded on her forehead. Titania radiated heat.

"Thank you," Titania said, embarrassed.

"You're welcome!" Luna replied, trying to play it off as no big deal. She really didn't mind helping. She couldn't wait for Titania to meet others like her. Luna knew it would be so good for her.

"We should be there by nightfall," Luna told her encouragingly. "Just a little further."

Titania gave her a strained but genuine smile.

As the sun began sinking into the West, Luna noticed Titania's breathing getting more and more ragged. She hoped it was just the atmosphere change. The temperature was dipping rapidly and had a bite to it. This fall air was enough to make anyone's airways a little irritated.

Luna started talking to try and keep Titania alert. She told Titania about the cave and the Titans. Titania nodded, listening politely.

"I think you'll really like Adam. He's really smart. I got an illness only canines can get, and he was able to help me, even while I was sick in human form, and then there is…" Luna halted.

Titania collapsed onto the ground.

NO!

Luna bent down. She looked worriedly ahead. She wasn't about to lose this girl. They were maybe a mile from the cave. Luna checked her head for bumps, finding nothing. Titania's breath was more stable than it had been, but it was shallow. Luna pulled down her sleeves to cover her hands and scooped Titania up. She started running. She wouldn't be able to hold Titania for long without being burned.

She gave it everything she could. Luna considered trying to transform partially to give herself more speed, but she had never done that before. She didn't know if she could isolate her transformation like that. And she didn't want to risk dropping Titania trying.

Her lungs burned. Her legs felt like jello. Even though Titania wasn't huge, the exhaustion of their trip weakened Luna considerably.

Luna breached the rocks surrounding the cave, falling to her knees. The gaping hole going down into the earth was a sight to behold. She set Titania down a few feet from the edge. With her remaining strength, Luna transformed. She gave a low, eerie howl. She transformed back to human, then laid down beside Titania and waited.

§

Within minutes, a six-foot-long lizard clung to the walls of the cavern. Luna heard the quick steps as it bounded over the ridge of the top. A large eagle ascended on white wings, its talons grasping Titania. The sunset barely illuminated them as Luna clung tightly to the back of the lizard Titan. It held onto the walls of the cavern, descending them into darkness.

Isaac, the eagle Titan, lowered Titania onto the floor of the cave. As soon as Luna dismounted the lizard Titan, she rushed to Titania's side. Another Titan, a girl with cat whiskers embedded in her face, brought Luna a solar lantern. It illuminated most of the room of the cave. Luna set it down beside Titania, causing shadows to extend beyond all the Titans standing, looking on at them.

The crowd of Titans spoke in hushed tones in a half-circle, watching the whole scene. Some were fully human, some fully animal, and a few unfortunate souls were neither.

"What's her deal?" Isaac, now in the form of a normal sixteen-year-old boy, asked as he pointed to Titania. He shook his hands in confusion, even though it was his talons that had been burned.

"I'm not sure," Luna explained truthfully. "Where's Adam?" She had no idea how far back into the cave system they had made camp in this place now, and she didn't want to waste time trying to hunt for him.

Trevor, the lizard Titan, pointed to just beyond the small crowd.

There, a tall man with mussed hair strode in briskly, his brow set. His expression made him look well older than his eighteen years, in Luna's opinion. Her heart fluttered with anxiety. How would he take this? Would he be mad at her? She had come later than she had promised, and she had brought a perfect stranger, but she liked to believe any of them would have done the same to help another Titan.

The crowd parted for him, as though they had a choice. The solar lamps strewn throughout the cave only served to dramatize his features. He glanced at Luna, then at Titania, his expression unreadable.

"Bring her back," Adam instructed calmly. He picked up the lantern and headed down the main corridor. The Titans watched, glancing curiously at Titania.

Luna gave Isaac a pleading look that asked without words for him to carry her. Isaac responded with a sigh.

"Make the bird carry what the wolf brings in, I see how it is," he said. His wink told Luna that he meant it good-naturedly. He tugged down his sleeves to give his arms the least bit of protection and gingerly picked up Titania's unconscious form.

Luna fell into step beside Adam, while Isaac followed behind.

"You're late," Adam whispered under his breath.

"I'm sorry," Luna apologized. "Things didn't quite go as planned."

"I gathered," Adam said.

He dipped into a room with a few makeshift cots on the floor.

Isaac set Titania down on one, but quickly lifted her back up when smoke started rising from beneath her.

"Just set her on the floor here," Adam pointed.

"Okay," Isaac replied. "But next time she has to be moved, you're picking her up." He laid her down where Adam indicated.

"Can you help her?" Luna dared to ask.

"We're about to find out, aren't we?" Adam said, cracking open his bag from the corner of the room.

CHAPTER TWENTY-FOUR

Adam ruffled through his bag, his face tight. Luna fidgeted nervously, unsure of what to say.

"Were you followed?" he asked.

"No," Luna said. "I made sure of it."

"I hope you're right."

Adam pulled a wand-looking instrument out of his bag and fiddled with a switch on the side. It began putting out a subtle green glow. He passed it over Titania's body, apprehension apparent. It began beeping wildly. The glow turned bright red. Luna's hands flew to her ears. It was so loud!

"She's got a tracker!" Adam said frantically, eyes wide.

"What?" Luna hissed. "How is that possible? I checked her while she was out!"

Adam wasn't quick to answer her question. Instead, he began isolating the wand over her legs, then her arms, and her neck. It was beeping and red no matter where he placed it.

"It's not a chip, it's a blood-contaminant tracker," he groaned.

"What do we do?" Luna's face felt hot. She hadn't wanted to put anyone in danger. She didn't want to let everyone down trying to save Titania. And she definitely didn't want Adam upset with her.

"I've got some chelators that might disable it, if it's the type I think it is." Adam dug into his bag again.

Frustrated, he dumped it out onto the floor of the cave. The smooth ground made empty vials roll until they hit the nearest wall. He didn't seem to notice or care; he was hyper-focused on the chelators.

Adam picked up a few small glass bottles and inspected them.

"How long has she been like this?" he asked as he prepared a syringe of the contents.

"I don't know," Luna admitted. "I think for quite a while. She mentioned she was a child when they changed her. She seems to have escaped soon after."

Adam raised an eyebrow.

"How has she escaped being captured for this long with a tracker in her?" he asked incredulously.

Luna winced as she watched Adam inject the chelate into Titania's bloodstream through her inner elbow.

"You'll have to ask her," Luna said. "I don't know. I know she was in a compound, apparently without raising suspicion, up until about a week ago."

Adam furrowed his brow.

"We'll see if this takes," he said. "We'll give it about twenty minutes and check it again. In the meantime, you'll need to tell the others she's got a tracker so they can prepare for whatever may come."

Luna's face flushed with shame. She knew it was her responsibility. She nodded and turned to go.

"Luna?" Adam called.

"Yeah?" She turned, staring down at the damp corner of the cave rather than meeting his gaze.

Adam cleared his throat. He stayed silent until she met his eyes.

She felt like he was boring a hole into her soul.

He removed the space between them, looking down at her.

"Don't do that again," he said sternly.

Before she could react, he collapsed into her with a hug.

"You scared me," he whispered, his breath hot on her neck.

Luna stood, awkwardly squished under his weight, but her spirit was dancing freely again.

Adam wasn't mad at her. Or at least, not that mad. It was going to be okay. They would figure all of this out.

CHAPTER TWENTY-FIVE

James.

James?

James!

Titania tried to run to him, but her legs wouldn't move. Why wouldn't they move? She tried to swing her arms faster. Maybe that would help!

"Don't do that," a voice laughed.

That's not James. Titania frowned.

She tried to turn around.

"Hey now," the voice said again, "You're going to rip out your IV, and then what are we going do?"

IV? What?

Titania blinked her eyes open. A red and brown swirled stalactite hung from the ceiling directly above her, its long shadow cast onto the wall by the warm yellow glow of a solar lamp. She scrambled, trying to push herself backward as though it would impale her.

"Hey!" A man coaxed her, his black hair and dark eyes hovered just above her. He put a gentle hand on her arm. "You need to take a deep breath for me."

"No, don't!" Titania sat upright and pushed herself away from him to break away from his touch.

His skin was warm. She could feel it. What she couldn't feel was the familiar fire scorching her flesh. The dawning realization filled her with confusion. She looked down at her arms, turning them over. They were her usual color of healthy pale with a touch of olive.

"What's going on?" Titania asked. "Where is James?"

A wave of panic rushed over her. Had Silen gotten her, too? Was this a makeshift hideout of his? She couldn't remember much but running.

"If you've hurt him," she growled at the man before her.

"Whoa!" The man held up his hands in surrender. "I don't know a James. Luna brought you here to get you help for your... DNA merging."

Titania's head swam. Luna... Luna... Her thoughts came slowly and with much effort. Was this the doctor Luna had told her about?

"Is that why my skin is normal?" Titania asked, dragging her IV roughly forward as she checked her legs. "Did you fix it?"

"I can only give you a temporary reprieve," the man cautioned. "I've given you an immunosuppressant that works on DNA spliced individuals. What that means is that, for now, your body isn't fighting against one DNA or the other. It'll work while you are on it, and maybe for a bit afterward. It's not a permanent fix. You still need to find a way to integrate your DNA sets, but some of the other Titans may have some more ideas for you on that. I'm just the doc. My name is Adam."

He gave her his hand to shake. She reluctantly took it, looking him up and down. Titania had a hard time taking it all in. She felt like she was dying, only to be brought back and told she had more work to do.

"It's nice to meet you," Titania told him politely.

"It's nice to meet you too, Titania. Luna has already told me quite a bit," Adam said with a smile. "All good, of course. I did have a few questions for you, if you feel up for it?"

"Sure," Titania agreed, though she felt far from up for it. The more she spoke, the rougher her throat felt. It was dry and scratchy. She shifted uncomfortably.

"You can stretch your legs if you want." Adam offered a hand to help her up.

She took it, still in awe that she could touch another human and not burn up. Titania pushed against the pile of clothes on the floor that made up her cot and stood. Her legs felt weak, as though they were made of jello.

"So," Adam broached, "I don't mean to alarm you, but you had a tracker in your blood. Do you know anything about that?"

Titania's knees had felt like they were going to give up from lack of use before she got that news. Now she thought she might collapse altogether.

"A what?"

She shivered. That made for another violation at the hands of Silen.

"A tracker. I know the trackers they used to show in movies were like microchips, but there are more subtle ones that exist now. They were originally designed to track down Titans that might abandon their mission. If one ran or otherwise defied their orders as a soldier, they could be easily tracked down and... dismissed." Adam gulped. "They are microparticles that circulate through your body, undetectable to you or anyone that doesn't have a tracking receiver. Some are activated by certain programmed signals. For the most part, they are almost impossible to remove. However, I was able to successfully deactivate yours."

"Thank you," Titania said gratefully, as a roller coaster of emotions swept through her.

Rage. Exhaustion. Pain. Grief.

The worst part of this whole thing was that she would never be separated from everything Silen had done to her. She'd never be able to get the traces of being a science experiment out of her body. She struggled to inhale, as though the air had been ripped right out of the room.

Adam reached out and held her arm to help steady her. "It's ok. I presume you didn't know. I am sorry to have to be the one to break such news."

"I definitely didn't know," Titania said, guilt plaguing her. Had she placed Luna and Adam in danger by allow-ing Luna to take her here? Was she to blame for James' kidnapping? Is this how Silen had found her?

"I'm so sorry for putting you in danger." Titania's eyes watered.

"Think nothing of it." Adam brushed it aside with the wave of his hand. "If we don't have each other's back, who will?"

"Thank you," Titania smiled through the tears spilling down her cheeks.

She felt so stupid, standing in the middle of a cave crying. The acoustics of the cavernous room amplified her quiet sobs.

"I had one other question for you," Adam said, seeming as though he was reluctant to ask while she was in the middle of crying.

"Of course," Titania said, wiping away the tears. "What is it?"

"I've seen a lot of things," Adam broached, "but never anything quite like your skin in transformation. Would you be opposed to me doing a test to see what you were spliced with?"

Titania's emotional overload only increased. Could she know what she was? Could he really do that?

"If you're not comfortable with it," Adam said, "I, of course, understand."

"No, no," Titania assured him. "Yes, I'd love to know. I was wondering if—"

"Hey!" Luna said as she turned the corner into Titania's makeshift room. "You're up! How are you feeling?"

Luna stopped in her tracks when she realized Titania was wiping away tears.

"Oh," Luna looked at Adam for help. "What's the matter?"

"Thank you so much for getting me help," said Titania. Emotions overwhelmed her.

"Of course!" Luna said, walking to her to give her a quick side hug. Titania flinched, which caused Luna to check to make sure she wasn't touching her IV.

"Can I go get James, now?" Titania said, hopeful.

Luna frowned. "I'm not sure you're in any condition to do that yet…"

Titania caught a glimpse of Adam shaking his head left and right at Luna.

"I've heard a bit about your friend, James," Adam soothed. "I think it would be good for you to be able to fight at full capacity before you go after him. Just because, well, you don't know what you could be up against when you find him, yeah?"

Titania looked down, trying not to let the tears come in another violent wave.

"He's right," Luna said. "You would scare the pants off of anyone even not fully transformed, but you'll have a lot easier of a time getting James back if you can integrate first."

Titania considered what would happen if she just left right now. Ripped the IV out of her arm, ran for the nearest exit, and flew out as fast as she could. But she already felt fatigued just thinking about it, let alone trying it. Could she even transform with the immunosuppressant on board?

"Okay," she reluctantly agreed. She resolved to herself that she wouldn't wait long to leave, even if Adam and Luna didn't like it. Even if she wasn't fully integrated. She would go after James.

She'd get him back.

CHAPTER TWENTY-SIX

Luna watched Titania carefully as she interacted with the other Titans. She was so glad to see her in better spirits and off of the IV. She seemed to be recovering quickly, which was promising. While only a single Titan had grumbled about the discovery of Titania's tracker, Luna still felt bad. She wanted to make sure they could all make it out if that Silen guy had found their location before the tracker was disabled.

Once Titania got over the fact that they were in a cave, she seemed to relax quite a bit. Luna couldn't blame her. It was unnerving to be surrounded by dark, enclosed walls all of the time. The poor girl was a bundle of nerves without that boyfriend of hers. She hoped Titania would find her strength, even in his absence. That was the only way she could see Titania mastering her transformation.

Luna shook her head, bemused. The cat Titan, Miranda, was showing Titania all her tricks.

Miranda, bless her heart, had been spliced with a cat. And Miranda was allergic to cats. She rarely went fully human, because if she did, it caused her to sneeze uncontrollably. Instead, she opted to keep the whiskers and cat nose on her facial features. It mitigated the allergy without being too visually disturbing.

"This is how I transform," Luna overheard Miranda say to Titania. "Are you ready?"

Titania nodded her head vigorously, as though this was just a normal show and tell time at a kindergarten class.

Miranda morphed to fully human, her whiskers disappearing, and let out a loud sneeze that hunched her over. When her head came up, she instantaneously shook out her fur as a full-fledged calico cat. Hair and dander flew into the air, like little pieces of fluffy confetti. She was larger than a normal house cat, despite having been spliced with one. She was closer in scale to a medium-sized dog. Just big enough to raise a bit of confusion, but not scary enough to have the same visual impact as, say, a tiger.

"Wow!" Titania said, impressed. "I'll be able to transform that effortlessly?"

"Probably!" Miranda said encouragingly, changing back to her mostly human self. "It just takes a bit of practice."

"Yeah," Trevor bragged as he ran a hand through his spiky hair. "Watch this!"

He ran at the wall, changing into his giant lizard form just before he would have impacted it. Instead, he scaled it, his sticky feet clinging to the beveled surface with no effort. Titania looked on in awe, surprised that he could hang on to the slick terrain.

"She seems to fit in just fine," Adam said to Luna, sidling up next to her.

"Sure does!" Luna grinned, relieved that bringing Titania here was working out. It was always a little nerve-wracking to see how rescues would integrate, but Titania was admittedly a different scenario than normal.

"Seems like everyone is enjoying having someone to show off to as well," Adam chuckled.

He was right. Most of them hadn't been impressed by one another. They had each already known of the existence of other Titans by the time they were free. But Titania wasn't like them. She had been alone, not knowing that she had a family just like her, just outside the safety of the government's clutches. In time, Luna knew she would thrive with the freedom of the outside and the community that they had in each other.

Truthfully, she wasn't sure that Titania getting back to James was a good idea. He wasn't like them. She knew the other Titans likely wouldn't accept him. And Titania would have to be forced to choose between them.

Isaac flew just below the opening of the cave, leaving a shadow from the natural sunlight on the floor in the shape of an eagle. Titania looked up in a trance. Luna couldn't imagine having been alone for so long like Titania had. People, like wolves, were pack animals after all.

Isaac landed in the middle of the floor.

"That was amazing!" Titania gushed.

"Well thanks," Isaac gave her a cheesy grin. "It's pretty easy. I love having wings!"

"Should we get to training so that Titania here can start using hers?" Adam suggested.

"Sounds like a job for me." Jen stepped out from behind Luna and Adam.

"That's a good idea," Luna said, encouraging Titania. "Jen had a really hard time at first, she's the best person to help you."

Titania nodded to her. Jen was no nonsense. She had barely given Titania more than a 'hi' since she'd arrived.

"How do you transform now?" Jen jumped right into it.

"When someone touches my skin, it burns and spreads from there. Right now, with the medicine on board, it isn't doing that, though," Titania said.

Jen frowned.

"What happens when you try to transform on your own?"

Titania looked to Luna for reassurance. Luna nodded at her.

"I haven't tried," Titania admitted. "It's kinda painful and I can't make it go away. Since I've always kept it a secret, it seemed counterintuitive to make it happen."

"Sounds like you know what we need then." Jen crossed her arms. "An incentive."

Titania looked at Jen, perplexed. Luna could understand that. She wasn't sure she could come up with an incentive if she were in Titania's shoes.

"What do you want?" Jen pressed her. "What could you do if you had control of this?"

Luna knew instantly what Titania's answer would be.

Titania's eyes lit up.

"Good, you got something?" Jen said, "You don't need to tell me. Just think of it, think of the energy it brings to consider it. Then use that energy. Circulate it through your body."

Titania looked like she was concentrating hard. Her brows furrowed, eyes clamped shut.

"Can you feel it?" Jen asked excitedly.

Titania exhaled, "No."

Jen didn't miss a beat.

"That's okay," she said. "There is more than one way to skin a cat… no offense to Miranda."

Miranda snarled at her, nonetheless. Titania giggled, but upon seeing Jen's stern face, she focused her attention on the training again.

"This isn't a long-term strategy," Jen warned. "But it may help in a pinch until we can get this figured out. Everyone has something different that works for them. Think of what scares you the most."

Titania thought for a moment, then nodded.

"Good, okay now," Jen instructed. "Think of that coming to pass or coming after you. Do you feel an energy attached to it? The adrenaline given to you to try and stop it? See if you can circulate that and force a transformation."

The Titans all took a step back, evidently believing that if something would take, it would be this. Luna wasn't sure that any of them hadn't used this trick, once or twice at least, in the beginning.

Titania's skin started glowing red.

"Yes!" Jen cheered. "You're getting there! Keep going!"

Steam came out of Titania's nose as she exhaled, lost in concentration.

She faltered and her flames fizzled out. Jen grabbed her by the arm to steady her.

"I'm sorry," Titania said sadly. "I feel really tired all of a sudden."

"That's okay," Jen assured her. "You've probably run your adrenaline dry over the last week. We may need to press pause on this and try again tomorrow. If we run you dry, it'll take longer and longer for you to get it."

Luna saw the frustration on Titania's face. She jumped in, "Jen is right. None of us learned this overnight! Now you know two things you can practice when you are feeling up to it. Besides, it's almost time to eat dinner."

Titania nodded, defeated.

"She'll get it," Jen mouthed to Luna and Adam. Luna was confident she would. She just didn't know how long it would take. Jen had experienced such difficulty with her transformations because of her animal mind, but none of them had gone through what Titania had. This was new territory, for all of them.

CHAPTER TWENTY-SEVEN

"AHHH!" James growled, wings slowly growing in between his shoulders.

He had a high pain tolerance, but growing these was slow and agonizing. The pain pulsed in dull aches, sharp stabbing sensations, and an otherworldly stretching. Had this been how it felt for Titania? Would his skin burn as hers had? And to think, she had been all alone, practically a baby when this had first happened. James saw red.

He lunged at the cage the guards had put him in, the idea of revenge pulsing in his head right along with the pain. James shook the cage with all his might. He was so angry; the metal gave way as he pushed on it.

A guard nearby smirked at his partner. They looked down on James as though he was a freak show exhibit at a circus.

"Face me!" James called out to Silen. That coward had fled the moment he thought James was a threat. He had ordered these guards to do his dirty work. Real men finished what they started. James knew all he needed to about Silen.

"If you know what's good for you," one of the guards bent down and squatted in front of James' cage, "you'd shut up, boy."

James snarled, knowing there was no way these guards were any older than him. He took a swipe at the man. The guard's partner pressed a button on a handheld device.

Electricity buzzed through the metal cage. Before James could think about it, the cage was electrocuting him from every angle.

"AGH!" he groaned, falling back and curling up into the fetal position.

"Not so tough now, are you big bird?" The guard taunted him, holding up one of James' feathers just outside the cage. It was two-toned; black from the quill through the middle, and white at the tip.

James glowered, the sort of glare a person wouldn't want to receive if looks could kill. He didn't care if they shocked him again. He didn't care about anything but that Titania was safe from these people now. That, and maybe making this crazy man pay for everything he had done to her.

James saw the guard's eyes go wide. He tipped his head to the side, waiting for an explanation, but none came. James glanced over, unable to see more than the tip of his still-small wings. What was the guard staring at?

He felt an unexpected tingle in his feet and looked down.

James' heart dropped into his stomach as he saw what the guard had seen.

CHAPTER TWENTY-EIGHT

Titania's cheeks flushed from exertion. She put her hands on her knees, struggling to catch her breath. Jen had been at this with her for three days and nothing that they had tried was working. All Titania had to show for her work were burns across her body and an ever-growing sense of agitation.

"Let's try this again," Jen said, squaring up.

Jen thought that maybe, if Titania was forced to protect herself, she'd be able to have some semblance of control over her transformation. But no matter how many swings she threw, no matter how many surprise sweeps of the leg she fell to, the most Titania could muster was a dull pillar of smoke from each hand as she blocked. The effort caused a transformation in various parts of her torso, but nothing substantial, let alone helpful.

Titania met Jen's punch, holding it in her hand.

"Ouch!" Jen winced, pulling away.

Titania saw the burn.

"I'm sorry!" Titania's eyes widened in sympathy.

"Don't be." Jen looked at her as though she had two heads. "This is what we want."

This wasn't what Titania wanted, but she nodded in acceptance anyway. What she wanted was to go get James.

Titania looked over to where the other Titans stood as onlookers.

Adam, Luna, Trevor, and Miranda were all chatting idly. Probably about something monotonous, Titania suspected. For being a bunch of runaway science experiments, she found it odd that they were all so relaxed. It seemed they didn't have a care in the world, like this cave was some kind of vacation spot.

And, she supposed, with them all working together, there wasn't much to worry about. Nothing they were bound to run into here was going to be something they couldn't all take together. They could scavenge and find small animals and berries to eat to sustain them. They had this special machine that filtered water, and the cave itself had enough tunnels and caverns that everyone who wanted one could have a private bedroom. They were set, really.

She could see the beauty in that, but at the same time, she didn't want to spend the rest of her life hiding in holes with them. She wanted James.

Jen took a quick swipe at her, knocking her leg out from under her. Again.

"Ooof!" Titania's lungs forcibly exhaled as she hit the floor.

Within an instant, Adam was beside her. He offered Titania a hand up, worry darkening his features.

"That was a little much, don't you think?" he questioned Jen.

She gave him a shrug. "Tough love. I'm just doing my job."

"I'm fine," Titania insisted, taking Adam's hand with embarrassment.

Truthfully, she felt like she'd bruised her entire back. But she wasn't willing to accept defeat. The sooner she got the hang of this, the sooner they'd let her go to James.

Adam's hands guided her to sit up. He inspected her back and sighed.

"You need another dose," he informed her. "Come with me."

Titania frowned. She would not continue to sit here in the bottom of a cave on emergency medicine to help her be 'normal' while she didn't know what condition James was in. Where was he? Was he even still alive?

She followed Adam reluctantly, running a bit to catch up with him. She almost knocked over some root vegetables being tested by their radiation sensor on her way and hastily apologized to the Titans managing the project.

"Has my DNA test come back?" she asked Adam as he drew up her medication and administered it into her IV port. Maybe if they knew that, they could speed this process up.

Adam chewed on his bottom lip.

"I checked against every known DNA sequence used in the Titan Project..." Adam explained.

"Any matches?" Titania cut him off impatiently.

"It didn't match any of them." Adam confessed.

He studied her, waiting for her response.

"So we still don't know what I am?" Titania said, frustration mounting.

Adam shook his head apologetically. She had hoped that finding out what she was would help them figure out how she could transform. Now that hope had evaporated.

She followed him back out into the common area, temper rising with every step.

"How am I ever supposed to get the hang of this?" Titania flung her arms down.

"Sometimes it can take a while," Adam assured her, "this integration process. Miranda had issues since she is allergic to cats. It took months to get her immune system to calm down so she could transform fully. She still has to work around it sometimes, you know?"

Titania's lips formed a thin, straight line. She didn't have months. This shouldn't have even taken the three days it already had. She wouldn't wait any longer.

"I don't have that kind of time," she growled, "I need to go now."

"I don't think..." Adam started, but she cut him off.

"I don't care." Titania's voice fell to a threatening, deep tone. "I'm done. I'm going after James. I'm of better use to him there than I am here, especially if integration could take months. There is no reason to wait any longer."

She fell silent as everyone turned to watch her outburst. Trevor and Miranda's smiles dropped. Luna and Adam shared a glance that Titania couldn't quite read.

"How are you going to find him?" Adam prodded, trying to make her see reason. "Do you even know which way he was taken?"

Titania's mind went blank from frustration. She knew where he had dipped into the woods, but after that? She had no idea. Luna had told her she knew, but what if she had only said that to get Titania to come with her?

"I do," Luna spoke up.

"What?" Adam turned to her in surprise.

"I know where they went," Luna clarified. "And even if he's not there anymore, I can track them by scent no matter where he's been taken since."

"You can't—" Adam argued with her.

"I can," Luna corrected him. Titania suspected he didn't want her taking Luna off on another grand adventure again.

Luna locked eyes with Titania and said firmly, "I'll go with you."

Titania stood in shock as Luna went to grab her travel bag.

"Let's think this through," Adam cautioned, motioning for them to slow down. "You two can't possibly take on a compound on your own."

Titania shrugged. "Depends on how you approach it, I'd wager. If we don't make a ruckus, it might be possible."

"What if they have tranquilizers?" he pleaded as Luna walked up. Titania suspected that was intentional.

Luna shuddered for a split second, but continued to pack up her things.

"Are you really going to leave out again?" Trevor asked Luna. "We just got settled in here, and we were planning a rescue mission for other Titans at the Clayton holding facility. This is just one human."

Titania was incredulous.

"Just one human?" she repeated in disbelief.

She paced in the center of the damp cave, light streaming down on her hair like a spotlight from the opening above. "What do you mean, just one human?"

"We've got to focus on our kind," Trevor asserted. "Humans won't be there for us! They think we're monsters. We need to spend our resources on our own. How do you know he's even still alive? How do you know this boyfriend of yours isn't in on creating Titans like us?"

"To be fair," Luna broke in, "I don't think they would tranq their own. He had been hit, I smelled it."

Trevor glared at her, unswayed. "They're savages. They'd do whatever they think will get them ahead."

"We're still human," Titania corrected him, spinning around to look at the Titans surrounding her. "We all are."

Miranda looked at her skeptically, her whiskers prominently displayed on her face.

"Don't you remember what life was like before?" Titania argued. "The simplicity of everyday things? Do you not feel the same empathy for people now? Do you not have the same desire for love and compassion? Do you not remember the sense of confusion you felt when you were injected? When you first transformed? How scary it was? How violated you felt? Just because they took us and used us as science experiments doesn't mean they changed our core, our spirit. We're not lab rats, we're humans!"

"Technically…" Trevor started.

Miranda landed a blow to his stomach, stopping him in his tracks. Titania didn't care. Whatever he was going to say, it didn't matter. She knew she was right.

"There are good humans and bad humans, but that doesn't mean all humans are bad. That doesn't mean that they are worth less than us. That doesn't mean he… James… isn't worth saving. He's my friend. My best friend," Titania finished.

A murmur fell over the crowd of Titans. Some bristled at her speech. Isaac flew to perch on a tall stalagmite, watching over the anxious room.

"We can't split up," one of the Titans complained. "What if we lose contact?"

"We could all go together," Luna said, arms crossed over her chest.

"What do I get out of it?" A boy Titania hadn't interacted with much asked. "What do I get for risking my life for this boyfriend of yours?"

Titania paused.

"We can stop the ones we encounter from hurting any-one again," she reasoned. "We can take out some of the people responsible for doing this to us. Not only to pro-tect ourselves in the meantime, but any future victims as well. An ounce of prevention is worth a pound of cure, right? You guys have been going to save Titans who have already been turned, but this would create less work for you in the future. This will give us an opportunity not just to rescue, but to prevent more rescues from being necessary."

The murmurs became louder until Adam's voice piped up from the cacophony.

"We'll go," he said with a sigh, pinching the bridge of his nose.

"What?" Trevor said incredulously.

"I said," Adam's words echoed through the cave, "we'll go. Everyone get ready, we'll leave within the hour!"

§

Luna slung her pack over her shoulder and waited for her ride up the glistening cave wall. Adam stood beside her, a blank expression on his face.

They looked back at Titania, who was assisting the re-maining Titans with packing their travel belongings. She bent down and hugged a girl with a permanent tentacle arm who was staying behind with Jen and some others who weren't suited for this mission. Titania was smiling and chatting with her as if it was the most normal thing in the world to have a tentacle arm. Luna knew there would be holdouts, but Titania worked well with almost all of the Titans in their group. She was a natural leader.

"Are you sure about this?" Trevor asked Adam before preparing to take him to the top.

Adam exchanged a knowing glance with Luna before answering.

"That girl is unstoppable," Adam said with a wry smile, "and I'd rather be fighting for someone like that rather than against them."

CHAPTER TWENTY-NINE

James turned in a circle, his feet itching. The fur growing on them was obnoxiously itchy. It took everything in
him to focus on his immediate threat instead of scratching. Guards armed with tranqs and stun batons hassled
him from every angle, taunting him and throwing things
at him.

"What'd they give you?" one of them yelled, "Pixie
DNA?"

The wings on his back were still small and didn't seem
to do much but feel tight against his shoulders. James kept
his cool and rustled them a little. He didn't care about
some bozo hurling childish insults. He just needed to figure a way out of this mess.

The guards had him surrounded, their shields forming
a barricade to keep him away from them. They randomly
tried to strike him with their weapons, attempting to pro-
voke him. James leaned back sharply, trying to dodge an

incoming attack. For the most part, he was successful. They had been at this for over half an hour and they'd barely grazed him. But this time, he was too slow.

The impact pushed the air out of his lungs and nearly landed him on the ground. The guards advanced on him, but he righted himself, hanging on to the weapon the man used to attack him. James made eye contact with the guard, a smirk creeping onto his face. His adversary realized too late what he was about to do.

James pushed the weapon back on the man, causing him to fall to the floor. Everything flew into chaos as he lunged toward the guard to continue his attack. Another guard caught him by the shoulder. James spun on him and landed a punch to his stomach.

The guard's eyes flared with rage. He grabbed James by the front of the shirt, lifted him up, and threw him onto the floor.

James brushed the back of his head quickly, trying to get the pain of the impact to subside.

"Not so tough now, are ya, boy?" The guard stood over him, a satisfied smile on his face. The other guards joined in on the pile on, spewing insults.

James suddenly had a hard time distinguishing which voice to focus in on. He felt like his ears were being pulled in every direction. Was it because he had hit his head? Did he have internal bleeding?

He looked up at the man who had landed him on the ground, adrenaline fueling his vengeful glare. But before he could mount an attack, his opponent's expression startled him.

The man looked confused, like he was studying James. He was looking at James' mouth. Had he lost a tooth? James put his hand to his teeth, feeling along them. He didn't notice that any were gone...

But they seemed bigger, maybe?

"His eyes!" one guard cried out. "Look at his eyes!"

James was so confused. Had he gotten a concussion? What were they talking about?

He moved to get up, but the guard above him knelt and landed a tranquilizer dose straight into his bicep. His arm stung. His head ached. And the room was a fuzzy static black.

CHAPTER THIRTY

"Ugh!" Trevor complained, "How much longer?"

Adam cast a disapproving glance his way.

"What?" Trevor pushed out his bottom lip. "I'm tired. I'm hungry, I'm thirsty, I'm…"

"Insufferable?" Adam offered.

Trevor glared at him, shutting his mouth.

Titania giggled. She couldn't help it. The way some of the Titans interacted with Adam reminded her of children exasperating their fathers with endless complaints and requests. Adam was long-suffering with all of them, but it didn't stop him from being quick-witted, too.

Their journey had been several days long, so she didn't blame Trevor for complaining. Titania's feet hurt considerably, and her burns were worsening now that she wasn't getting the regular immunotherapy. Adam had elected to leave the valuable supplies with those who had stayed at the cave. The immunotherapy, in particular, was something they definitely didn't want to lose on the journey. He'd only brought a single dose, but she hoped to not have to use it.

"What if lover boy isn't even there?" Trevor asked, failing to keep his mouth shut.

"Then I'll track him," Luna countered. "We've been over this."

"Didn't you say you thought they were taking him to a holding facility?" Trevor asked Luna.

"Yeah," Luna said. "Why?"

"So this guy is going to have seen the worst of this stuff?" Trevor said, directing his attention next to Titania. "What makes you think he's going to want to stay with you now that he's probably seen how we're made? Don't you think that'd be a little much for a puny human to process?"

Titania faltered, stunned at his harsh words.

"Trevor..." Luna chastised him.

"What?" Trevor said. "I'm just being realistic! If I was still human, I wouldn't be with someone that wasn't. For one, being intimately familiar with the difference, I know they wouldn't understand."

"James knows what I am, and he chose to continue on together anyway," Titania murmured.

"Maybe he didn't want to abandon a freak to the wilderness by herself," Trevor hissed. "Have you considered that?"

"Have you considered shutting up?" Adam asked him.

Trevor fell back toward the rear of the group, pouting like a wounded puppy.

"Don't pay him any mind," Adam assured Titania. "He's just ticked off that his personality would keep him perpetually single even if he was fully human."

Luna burst out laughing, nodding in agreement.

Titania smiled appreciatively. But the seed of doubt had already taken hold in her mind. Had James been sticking with her for pity? Or necessity, since it wouldn't be good for either of them to be alone in the wilderness?

Luna saw the downcast look on her face.

"What's the matter?" she asked.

"What if he's right?" Titania's anxiety spiraled. She felt a little silly confiding that kind of fear in someone she'd known for less than two weeks. But outside of James, Luna and Adam and their band of misfits were all she had in the world.

"Right about James?" Luna clarified.

"Yeah," Titania said solemnly. "What if James was just taking pity on me?"

Luna laughed. "I don't think so. I saw the way he looked at you. He might be a little freaked out by all this, but he genuinely cares about you."

Titania bit her lip to hide her smile. That was a relief to hear.

"We'll be there within the hour!" Adam announced to the group.

A few Titans in the back groaned, some in frustration and others in relief. This had been a long journey.

Titania barreled ahead with newfound energy, bounding like an overly excited puppy. They were so close! She would see James again soon and get him away from Silen.

Luna caught up to her, smiling cheerfully.

"Hey," she said, "there's something we should probably talk about before we get there."

Luna pulled away from the main group, motioning for Titania to follow her.

"Oh?" Titania asked, "What is it?"

"Well," Luna said carefully, "James might have seen more than just transformations and experimentation in the holding facility. There are some Titans that just don't take to the foreign DNA well. Instead of joining together, one set overtakes the other. Usually, the human one does but in some cases…the animal does."

"Oh…" Titania said.

"It's not pretty," Luna followed up. "They basically have animal brains at that point. Those Titans can be really aggressive toward humans and sometimes they end up… being put down."

Titania's stomach flopped. "That's horrible."

"It is," Luna agreed, "But since James might have seen things like that, I think you need to prepare yourself for him to be a little shell-shocked. You and I have seen some pretty scary things, but this is the first time he has really encountered the worst of it."

"That's a good point," Titania muttered. She hoped that someday soon this would all be a crazy fever dream to her and James.

Luna smiled and changed the subject. "Are you excited? We're getting so close!"

"Very." Titania's eyes lit up. "Hey, I was wondering if I could ask you something about Adam?"

"Oh," Luna said, surprised. "Sure, what's up?"

"He knows a lot about all this, but he never said anything about being a Titan himself. Is he a normal human?"

"Oh." Luna was somber. "Um… It's not really my place to share too much, but Adam is a Titan like us. He just doesn't like to transform. I honestly haven't ever seen him do it. I know he has his reasons…"

"Oh, okay," Titania said. "I didn't mean to pry, I was just wondering."

Luna gave her a friendly smile.

"I'm going to go scout ahead," she said. "One last thing…"

"What is it?" Titania asked.

"When we get there," Luna instructed her, "Be very careful running into other Titans. They aren't all like us. Apart from the ones afflicted with animal mind that go berserk, some of them signed up for this. Some of them willingly had this done to them as part of working for the government. Don't trust or talk to any of them there, okay? Let Adam and I handle that."

Titania wondered how anyone could willingly sign up for this, knowing what it entailed. She had signed up, but she hadn't known what she was signing up for. And besides that, she was just a kid.

"Okay," Titania nodded, taking it all in. "I'll follow your lead."

"Good," Luna said, transforming. She nodded back to Titania as a wolf before running off into the distance.

CHAPTER THIRTY-ONE

Silen sat, spinning subtly back and forth on a padded arm-chair in his newly commandeered medical bay. He stared a hole into the silent tracker in his hand. He wished it would work. There had been a stable connection for such a long time. There was no reason for it not to work now that he could think of. Nevertheless, he had every confidence that she would be here. He just wished he knew when.

"Do you still think she'll come?" a junior officer asked curiously, peering over Silen's shoulder.

Silen curled his lip, a little offended that the boy was speaking out of turn. But he saw it as an opportunity to show a display of strength and confidence. This would all go according to plan, even if there were a few unexpected mishaps.

"Did you hear the way that boy spoke about her?" Silen asked the junior officer.

"Yeah," the officer responded. "Kinda lame."

Silen gave a heavy sigh.

"Well," Silen said with exasperation, setting the tracker down on the counter. "Lame or not, I personally saw the way he and the girl interacted. I have not a single doubt that she will come for him. We just need to make sure she makes it here before he finds a way to bust out to get to her. He's still weak, but his will is strong, especially when it comes to her."

"Aren't you worried she'll tear this place apart to get to him?" the junior officer asked.

"It's true that she is powerful. In actuality, she is the strongest Titan I have ever created. But, she is only one individual. They were traveling with someone else, but even if they both tried to take this place, they wouldn't be successful. That doesn't mean we have to let them know that, though," Silen rambled to the junior officer.

He didn't even know why he felt the need. Maybe years of being discarded and discounted had worn on him more than he thought. It was nice to be well regarded and asked questions.

"She'll come," Silen's voice was laced with unhinged glee, "I have no doubt, she'll come back for him."

CHAPTER THIRTY-TWO

Luna returned, her paws padding on the washed-out gravel road.

Adam walked ahead to meet her as she transformed back to human.

"There." Luna pointed at a stark white compound to the East.

Like most other facilities designed by Lumis, it was single story and comprised of brick. The gravel road they trod extended to run past the compound on the North side, which was the only one visible because of the woods that surrounded it.

"They're still here. I smell them," Luna went on, crinkling her nose.

"Are we ready?" Adam asked everyone.

"I guess," Trevor grumbled, turning to Titania. "You're gonna seriously owe us for this."

Titania winced, but brushed it aside. She already knew she owed them for this. She owed them for saving her, too. And she intended to pay back her debts to them, whatever that might look like.

"As much as I hate to divide the group," said Adam, continuing to address them all, "we're probably going to need cover for our escape. This is not a scorched earth mission—we're not here to level the place. In and out. We rescue who we can, priority is James, and then we bug out. I need some of you to stay here and guard our retreat."

He picked out six Titans to remain behind.

Titania watched them preemptively transform as her own group pushed forward. She wished she could do that. She would feel a lot more equipped going into this if she could. A nagging sense of failure gnawed at her stomach. What if everyone else did all the work on her behalf, just because she couldn't get the hang of transforming?

She moved to the front of the pack where Luna and Adam walked. She wasn't going to let anyone take the hits for her. She would be an equal member of this team.

The group approached the compound by walking in the ditch to the right of the road. It allowed them to take advantage of the cover from the trees. When they drew nearer, Luna threw her arm out, stopping them all short of full view of it.

"There's a camera!" she hissed. "There!"

Titania looked to where she was pointing. An owl sat on the top of the roof. Was that what Luna was talking about? Titania thought it looked like a normal owl.

Adam stepped back slowly, wanting to make sure he wasn't in view of anything. A twig snapped beneath his feet, and the owl's head swiveled directly at them. He ducked into the woods, dragging Titania with him by the arm.

Luna transformed without anyone noticing and pretended as though she had been the one to make the sound. She trotted along after a brief moment of tension, catching up with the rest of the Titans now hiding in the woods.

"That was close," she breathed, changing back.

"Do you think it saw us?" Titania asked nervously, hiding the burns now forming on her arm in response to Adam's touch.

"No," Luna said, "I think we're alright. I don't think they'll come out to check anything either. They probably think I have rabies and I don't think they would want to risk that."

"We need to disable that thing or we won't be able to get in without getting captured," Adam said matter-of-factly.

"I agree," Luna said. "Any ideas?"

"We could send Trevor up," Miranda suggested. "He could climb straight up the wall and…"

"And what?" Trevor cut her off. "Eat that thing? They're gonna notice a giant lizard on the camera well before I can get to it."

Miranda sulked. "It was just an idea."

"What about Isaac?" Trevor offered, throwing his friend under the bus. "He can fly."

"I mean," Isaac said, "I'd be willing, but I'm not sure how I could escape the camera either. It'd be pretty weird for an eagle to just start attacking an owl. Owls have been known to attack bigger birds. So an eagle attacking an owl unprovoked might not seem like to most natural thing. I don't know, maybe I'm overthinking it?"

"Maybe so," Adam mused. "But I agree, subtlety might be a better strategy."

Adam looked over at the quietest Titan of the bunch and smiled. Titania had barely spoken with her since meeting everyone. She didn't even know what this one was spliced with because it seemed like she barely spoke at all.

"Natalie," Adam addressed her. "Would you be willing to help us out on this one?"

"What did you have in mind?" She was so soft spoken, Titania barely heard her.

The girl beamed at Adam, excited that he had called on her for something. Her shoulders hunched over. It looked like she was making herself smaller than she already was. She stood maybe five feet even, with tousled brown locks that hung in her face.

"Would you let Isaac pick you up and fly you up there? You could chew the cords without causing a scene. He could circle over you like he was trying to find an opportunity to catch you until you're done. Then he can bring you back down to us."

Natalie's face was unsure.

"I won't drop you," Isaac assured her. "Not hard, at least."

Natalie gulped and looked up at the roof of the compound.

"Maybe I could go up and melt it at the base?" Titania offered, not wanting this to fall on Natalie if she was too afraid.

"No," Natalie said quietly. "I've got this."

She started transforming, brown hair sprouting out of her skin. Titania watched her body shrink smaller and smaller until Natalie wasn't any higher than their feet. She squeaked and skittered around in her little mouse body.

Titania's heart raced. She hoped that Isaac really would be careful. Natalie was so small and fragile. Titania's palms got sweaty as she considered how badly this could go. She didn't want anyone to get hurt on her account.

"Ready?" Adam asked.

Natalie squeaked in response.

"Here goes nothing!" Isaac said.

He transformed, his nose taking on a beak-like quality.

Isaac grasped Natalie in his talons and took flight away from the facility. Titania watched him as he ascended into the sky and made a loop, now heading straight for the compound.

He shrieked as he flew over it, getting about a foot above the roof before dropping Natalie. She went rolling and, for a moment, Titania's heart stopped. Isaac landed and pretended to peck at her. She got up and skittered over to the owl.

Titania was able to follow the whole show with her eyes due to the slant of the roof. She squinted to see Natalie chewing at the wires under the owl. Isaac flapped his wings and started circling the sky, occasionally dipping down to try and see her better.

The owl's head was on a swivel as it struggled to keep up with Isaac. Titania thought it may have been a better plan to have him distract the darn thing the entire time.

Isaac made another pass, but the owl froze in place. It jerked its head a few times, struggling to move. Then it stopped moving entirely.

Natalie's tiny body skittered out from behind the owl. Isaac swooped down and picked her up. He flew her around in circles a few times before bringing her back to the woods.

They landed smoothly.

Isaac and Natalie transformed back into humans. They sat in the dirt, both gasping for air. They looked at each other and started laughing hysterically. Natalie tried to stand, but tipped over. Isaac caught her, laughing.

Isaac gave her a high-five. "We did it!"

"Don't ever spin me around like that again," she giggled.

"Good job!" Adam patted them both on the back.

Natalie beamed again, glowing from the praise.

Titania smiled at them. "Thank you."

"No problem," Isaac said proudly.

"That was actually kind of fun," Natalie agreed.

"We should get this show on the road," Luna suggested, cutting off the giddy, adrenaline-fueled celebration. "I don't know when they'll be coming out to fix that or how long it'll be til they notice."

Titania's smile faded. Luna was right. They needed to focus. James was within their grasp!

"We need to decide who will go in, and who will stay outside," Adam instructed. "A few of us need to stay right out here to monitor the security system and make sure we have a clean getaway. The rest of us need to go in prepared to transform and fight."

"Got it," Titania said.

"I'll stay out here," Miranda said. "I don't think you'll have much use for me."

"Me too," Trevor said. "I don't think there'll be much use for a giant lizard."

"I think I need a rest," Isaac said sheepishly. "That wiped me out."

"Very well," Adam said. "Natalie, Titania, Luna, and I will go in. You guys stay out here."

"Natalie, I hate to ask this of you," Adam continued, "but when we open the door, would you mind going in and creating a diversion somewhere so that we can get where we need to go without being seen?"

"Sure," Natalie agreed.

Titania was sure that being a mouse made her feel pretty unhelpful sometimes. It wasn't any wonder why she was so eager to help.

"If anything happens and we get split up," Adam instructed, "don't head back to the cave immediately. We want to be able to return there safely, not bring the government there hot on our heels."

"Yes sir," Isaac spoke for the group staying outdoors.

"Alright," Adam said. "Let's go."

Titania and Natalie behind followed Adam and Luna.

Titania's heart raced. She was so close to having James back.

Right before they reached the door, it swung out and open. They all jumped behind it.

"What the heck is going on!" A man stomped out with a ladder.

The Titans all froze in place. The man rounded the corner without noticing them, apparently too absorbed in his fuming.

"He must be going to fix the owl," Natalie whispered.

Adam let out a breath. "That was close. We need to hurry."

Natalie transformed and headed inside. A few anxious minutes elapsed as the others waited, listening as best they could through the barely cracked door. At last, she popped her head back out and squeaked at Adam, Titania, and Luna.

They followed her in.

Natalie ducked into an empty office, and the others followed. Adam closed the door as she transformed back to human.

"There's hardly anyone in here at all," Natalie said, confused. "It's like a ghost town."

"That should make our job easier, right?" Titania said.

Luna frowned. "That's a little suspicious."

"Keep a sharp eye out," Adam instructed.

He looked around the room and found a closet full of lab coats.

"Here." He handed one to each of them. "Put these on."

Titania slipped hers on, but with the burn on her arm, she knew it wouldn't be intact for long. Still, she didn't argue.

"Just act natural," Luna encouraged them. "We'll blend in like this."

The group stepped out of the room. They walked down the hallway, passing a few open, empty rooms and a few closed doors. When they passed the first room with an open door and staff members inside, Titania thought she might have a heart attack. But the people didn't even turn around.

She looked curiously at Adam, but his attention was focused straight ahead.

They came to a branch in the hallway.

"Which way do we go?" Natalie asked. She glanced back and forth between the path they were on and the new one.

"We'll go down this one," Adam motioned, indicating that he and Natalie would continue on the original hall-way. "Luna, take Titania down that way."

"Got it!" Luna said.

Adam and Natalie disappeared around the corner as Titania and Luna took a step into the new hallway. Luna sped along it like a woman on a mission, right as a boy about their age stepped out from a door and straight into her. Titania winced as they collided.

"Are you okay?" Titania asked her, bending down to help her up.

"I am SO sorry!" the boy apologized. "I didn't mean to run into you like that."

"It's okay," Luna waved them both off. "I'm fine."

"You were sure in a hurry," the boy teased her. "Have somewhere to be?"

"Oh I, um…" Luna mumbled.

The boy furrowed his brow. "Say, I don't recognize you. Either of you. Are you new here? I didn't know we were expecting trainees today."

The boy reached for a radio hooked on his belt.

Luna panicked. Before Titania could speak or do anything, Luna threw a punch at him, knocking him into the wall. Titania's eyes went wide.

He stumbled backward, holding his bleeding nose. What were they going to do? The boy opened his mouth to scream for help, but Luna lunged forward and covered it, eyes locked on his.

"Do not say anything if you want to live, do you understand?" she whispered menacingly.

The boy tried to push against her and fight back, but she was stronger.

His eyes looked her up and down in fear. She narrowed hers and pulled him back into the room he had come out of. Luna made quick work of gagging him, using strips of a medical gown to bind his hands and legs as Titania kept watch. This had NOT been part of the plan.

Titania heard footsteps down the hall.

"I hear somebody," she whispered to Luna.

Luna started transforming, ready for a fight.

Their new prisoner squirmed against his bonds as he took in her appearance. Titania closed the door and locked it behind her.

Seconds later, the handle jiggled.

"Brent?" a female voice came from behind the door. "Why is this door locked?"

Luna's eyes shot daggers at their captive.

Titania carefully walked over to him.

"Get her to go away," Titania whispered, "or my friend is gonna rip your throat out."

Luna snarled at him as Titania took out his gag.

"I'm having a little bit of trouble with a patient," Brent told the woman through gritted teeth. "I just needed to make sure they wouldn't escape. I've got it under control. I'll be out in a minute."

He glared at Luna and Titania.

"Okay..." the woman outside said hesitantly. "Call if you need help."

Titania put the gag back on before he could say another word.

She held her breath until she heard the woman's footsteps leave.

Luna turned back to human and brushed the remaining fur off of her clothes.

"Let's go," she walked to the door and unlocked it, not even bothering to look back at Brent.

Titania looked at him, almost sympathetically, before following Luna out.

"What if someone finds him?" Titania asked.

"They will," Luna said certainly. "But we'll be gone by then. It's not like they weren't going to notice James missing. They would've found out someone had been here one way or another."

Luna closed the door behind them and began speed walking down the hallway again. Titania caught up to her, glancing into each open door they passed.

Titania froze as they reached a closed door at the end of the hall. They heard voices on the other side.

"What do we do?" Titania whispered to Luna.

Luna held up a finger to her lips.

Titania nodded, falling silent.

"Just follow my lead," said Luna, boldly opening the door.

CHAPTER THIRTY-THREE

James' head hurt. He lay in his cage, curled up in the fetal position, dreading the next time they shocked him.

He clenched the small blue rock in his hand that he had taken from the stream after they escaped Lone Leaf. He still wore the same clothes, now travel-stained and torn, as he had then. Finding the rock still in his pocket had given him a small measure of comfort. It was all he had left of her now.

He heard the door open and flinched. Were they back to take him into another torture circle? He acted like he hadn't even noticed it until he heard Luna's voice. Could it be?

The young man standing next to James' cage started walking toward the door. James sat up and looked. It was Luna! How was she here? What was she doing? Oh no…

Titania.

She stood next to Luna, looking between her and the guards tasked with watching James. She shouldn't be here! Silen would take her too! He wanted to scream at her to run, but he knew that would set off his captors. As it stood, it seemed like Luna was sweet-talking them just fine.

"I'll just need to see your clearance card," James heard one of the young men say.

Luna didn't like that, and she let them know with the sweep of a leg. James' least favorite guard hit the floor with a satisfying smack, groaning and cursing.

The other moved to aim a tranquilizer. Titania reached out and grabbed his arm, burning it.

The guard sucked in air to try to ease the pain. Titania advanced on him, kneeing him in the stomach. Luna pried the tranq out of his hand and injected it into him. The young man's eyes widened as he weakly fell to the floor.

The guard Luna had dropped first climbed to his feet and tried to grab her from behind, putting his arm around her neck. She struggled against him. Titania looked shocked, like she didn't know what to do. Desperate to escape, Luna started transforming her head and bit into the man's arm with her wolf teeth. She slipped out of his grasp with ease.

He held his arm in shock. Luna spun around and decked him in the face. He fell to the floor, out cold.

James felt like he was in a fever dream, watching a girl with the head of a wolf take out the people who had been torturing him for days. It didn't feel real.

Titania dropped down to open his cage. She was so close. He could smell her. She looked normal except for her right hand. And healthier than he had seen her in a while. What had happened?

He watched her glance at the other two cages in the room. She eyed the people inside them nervously. James didn't blame her. He was suspicious that some of them had lost their minds. He could understand that though, he felt close to it himself.

Titania returned her attention to the lock, fumbling with it in her excitement.

"It's locked. I need a key!" she said frantically.

Luna searched the unconscious guard's pockets.

"Here they are." The keys rattled as she handed them over. "Let the other ones go too."

Titania gulped. Her hands shook as she searched through the keys to find the right one. Finally, one went smoothly in and clicked when she turned it.

The cage door swung open and James climbed weakly out. Titania wrapped her arms around him. He was so happy to see her again; he didn't have the heart to tell her she was burning him.

"I hate to break this up," Luna said, plucking the keys from Titania, "but we'd better go."

Luna locked the young men she had knocked out in the same cage where they had kept James. Then she went to free the other two Titans being held. One was a teenage boy, and the other was a little girl. They looked at her, nodding gratefully.

James wished so much to buzz the now imprisoned guards with electricity, just once, but Luna was right. They needed to go.

The group rushed down the hall, not even trying to quiet their footsteps.

"Do we need to go find Adam?" Titania asked Luna.

Who was Adam?

"No," Luna responded. "He knows the drill. He's probably already outside."

Titania nodded.

James had questions, but they would have to wait until they were safely out of here.

They reached the front door without incident, which he thought was weird. Where was everyone?

Luna swung the door open and ushered them out. James had to blink against the brightness.

He stepped out into the outdoors.

Into freedom.

CHAPTER THIRTY-FOUR

From just outside the front door, Luna looked left to the edge of the woods. There, Miranda's face peeked out, just visible. Luna let out a sigh of relief.

A mouse scurried out near the door and grew into a human.

Luna fell backward, almost bumping into Titania. "Natalie! You scared me!"

"Where is Adam?" Natalie asked her.

"What do you mean, he was with you?" Luna said. Her heart dropped.

"He told me to go outside and that he was going to go to get you. Did he not?" Natalie frowned.

"We haven't seen him," Luna replied, shaking her head.

"Then where…" Luna began, but the answer waltzed out from around the right side of the building.

"Good to see you again," Silen said.

Luna knew exactly who he was. His smell gave him away.

Two assistants trailed behind him, with Adam bound and held between them.

Luna lunged.

"Not so fast there, sweetheart," Silen said, holding up a hand to his assistants.

They held a tranquilizer to Adam's arm, hovering above his lab coat.

Luna froze in place. She did not want to fight with Adam out of commission. She knew she didn't have the firepower without him. Adam looked at her, his eyes filled with regret.

How had he gotten caught? Why hadn't he transformed? If there was ever a time to do it, it would be now!

Something caught her attention out of her peripheral vision. She turned to see Miranda and Trevor being herded toward them by other men and women in lab coats. Where was Isaac?

Luna's blood boiled. She knew that had gone entirely too well.

What were they going to do? She and Natalie were the only two not under active guard that could transform fully, and Natalie wasn't really helpful in a fight.

The others they had left behind! If Luna could transform into wolf and let out a howl to signal them, they could rush in and...

"Oh, and don't think your friends down the road will be of any use to you," said Silen, who must have perceived the growing hope on her face. "They've been detained since just after you left them there." His smirk was nauseating.

The teenage boy they had freed stepped out of the door behind them and her heart swelled with hope once again. Maybe he had a helpful skill! But the boy gave her an emotionless glance as he slid over to Silen, taking a place at his side.

"You're a traitor," Luna spat at him.

The boy smiled at her, a forked tongue coming out of his mouth. His eyes turned to slits. Luna stepped back, putting her arm out to protect Natalie, James, and Titania. The boy transformed into a snake, about five to six feet long and all black. He slithered up onto Silen's shoulders.

"I thought I'd lost you," Silen said, looking at Titania as though she were his long-lost daughter.

Titania glared at him, disgusted.

"When my tracker stopped working, I was a bit nervous. But I knew you'd come back for this boy of yours." Silen waved his hand dismissively at James. "I took good care of him for you."

Luna shivered uncontrollably. This man was out of his mind. How were they going to get out of here?

The little girl Luna had let out of her cage stumbled out of the door, rubbing her eyes. Luna pushed Titania, James, and Natalie back away from her. Luna wouldn't trust her even if she was on their side at this point.

That proved to be a wise decision when the girl joined the snake boy over with Silen. Luna sized up their odds.

With Isaac missing and Adam captured, they were out-numbered. And Silen had tranqs. This was not looking good.

"I must thank you for letting my assistants out," Silen said, wrapping his arm around the little girl. "I had so hoped you would. I hate getting my hands dirty."

Luna's muscles tensed. There was nothing they could do with Trevor and Miranda under guard on one side, and Silen and the evil Titans on the other, with an injection held on Adam's arm.

The little girl grew hair on her face. Her fingernails turned into claws. The nose of a bear replaced her delicate human one. At her full transformation, the girl was thankfully not the full size of a normal bear. It must have been because she was so young, Luna thought. She lumbered toward them. Natalie transformed down into a mouse and scurried away. One of the assistants tried to stomp on her, but he was unsuccessful.

"Restrain them," Silen ordered. "Don't let any more escape!"

The assistant holding Miranda placed shackles on her wrists.

Was this going to be it? Luna wondered. Had they come all this way to fail?

A shriek came down from the sky, startling every-one. An eagle descended on the assistants holding Adam, grasping at the tranq with its talon.

Isaac!

He plucked the tranq from the assistant's grasp and shrieked again as he ascended into the sky.

That was one problem out of the way.

Before Silen could react, Adam landed a punch to his stomach. Silen doubled over. The snake boy angrily coiled to attack Adam, but the assistants behind him pulled him back to try and thwart the attack. Had they been any slower, Adam may have been bitten in the face.

"Be safe," Luna said, looking back at James and Titania. "Take care of each other."

Luna's body folded down, hair spreading across it. Her spine contorted and claws protruded from her hands. She threw her wolf head into the sky and let out a howl before charging forward.

CHAPTER THIRTY-FIVE

James watched helplessly as Luna charged at the bear, viciously attacking it from every angle she could. The bear made swipes at her but each of them failed to land.

Behind them, the assistant holding the girl with the cat whiskers let out a yelp. James spun to see that the girl had transformed into a cat, slipping easily out of the shackles and landing several scratching blows to her handler.

The boy with the spiky hair took advantage of the distraction, shoving his handler before they could finish placing the shackles on his hands. He swung the shackle attached to his left wrist at the handler, hitting them squarely in the side of the head with the hard metal. The handler pulled up a tranq, but the boy jumped back and started running.

The bear noticed and abandoned Luna to chase after the fleeing boy.

"Alive!" Silen screamed, "I want them alive!"

James didn't know if the bear understood or cared about that.

He watched Luna divert to the assistants holding the older boy who had been saved by the eagle. She bounded toward them. The guy was putting up a good fight, but one of the handlers had managed to pull another tranq dose from their pocket and had it inches from his skin.

Luna put on the afterburners, but it was too late. The tranq found its mark, causing him to buckle. James could hear Luna whine. The snake coiled down Silen's arm, poised to bite her.

"Luna!" screamed James, trying to warn her.

She turned just in time to see the inside of the snake's mouth.

The eagle that had grabbed the tranq before swooped down, harrowingly snatching the snake in time.

The bird carried it higher and higher. The snake writhed angrily, snapping its jaws at the eagle. The pair was well over 100 feet in the air when the eagle dropped it. James figured it must have been trying to kill the serpent, because he didn't think it would survive from that height.

The snake sunk its teeth into the very bottom of the eagle's left leg. The eagle flew in circles, trying to shake it off.

Its wings slowed down, its circles becoming sloppy.

It lost momentum and descended to the ground, the snake still wiggling with its teeth sunk in.

"Oh no," Titania breathed out beside him. "He's poisoned."

James' eyes widened as the bird hit the ground. It didn't move. Commotion coming toward them caught his attention. The two assistants that had tranquilized the older boy were coming for them!

"Titania," James turned to her, "we have to get out of here."

She didn't move.

He grabbed her arms as her eyes filled with tears. "We need to go!"

This might be their only chance to escape. The bear was still occupied, now chasing a giant lizard, who was clambering up to the roof. The cat girl was keeping the other assistant busy chasing their own tail, trying to catch her.

Silen ran over to the snake and the eagle, pulling the snake out from under the bird.

James was sure it would be dead, but the snake wriggled back to life, slithering once again onto Silen's back.

James felt his hands burn, drawing his attention back to Titania, who he quickly released. She was on fire. He flinched back as her wings burst through the back of her lab coat and her skin began burning it to a crisp. He wished he could help. He wished he could fight as an animal like they did, but he didn't know how.

Titania let out a scream of pain, deafening everyone in the yard. They all crouched slightly at the sound and turned toward her.

None of them could look at her directly.
She was too bright.

CHAPTER THIRTY-SIX

It burned. Everything burned. It hurt so much.

Isaac was dead. It was all her fault.

She put herself in front of James, shielding him from the goons headed their way. She wouldn't let anyone else get hurt on her account. One of them shot a tranq at her, which she effortlessly caught in her hand, melting the middle of it. She turned and threw it back at him, hitting him in the upper thigh. The woman next to him faltered but kept moving toward her. This assistant pulled out a stun baton. Titania caught the blow, but the woman was strong. It forced Titania back and down.

Behind her, Trevor escaped down the side of the building, away from the camera repair man who was chasing him with a screwdriver. The man looked like he was going to jump down after him, but thought better of it and remained on the roof.

Freed of pursuit, Trevor crept behind the woman assaulting Titania and bit her on the leg, causing her to lose concentration. The woman tried to retaliate by hitting him with the bludgeon, but Titania grabbed the bottom of her arm, burning her and causing her to let go of it. This made it fall down much lighter than if it had been a full blow. It hit Trevor and rolled off his back. He shook the woman's leg, not appreciating that.

Titania heard a growl and a yelp and turned to see Luna losing her fight with the bear. It had made for the unconscious Adam after losing Trevor earlier, and Luna was all that stood in its way. Now Luna had several thin, bleeding gashes to her haunch.

"You got this one?" Titania asked Trevor.

The giant lizard nodded.

Titania took to the sky, her wings carrying her across the yard to where Luna was. She saw James out of the corner of her eye. He threw a solid punch at the handler terrorizing Miranda.

Titania descended behind the bear, wrapping her burning arms around its neck. The bear clawed at her arms, tearing off chunks of burnt flesh.

"AH!" Titania screamed, letting go. She looked down to see that pieces of her arms were gone. The bear knocked her back, and she tried to push herself away.

Luna lunged, grabbing the scruff of the bear's neck with her teeth.

It swiped at her, paws flying wildly.

Silen appeared in Titania's peripheral vision.

"I feel like I'm watching siblings fight," he said smugly, his arms crossed. "You are all kind of my children, in a way. My creations."

"I am not yours," Titania hissed, trying and failing to push herself up. "None of us are. We are our own."

"Without me," he bent down, leveling with her, "You'd be nothing."

He spat. The snake twisted out from behind his neck, eyeing her.

"Titania!" James cried. Her eyes widened as she struggled to back away on her shredded arms.

Before Silen realized it, the snake lunged at her, its teeth bearing down on her neck.

"NO!" Silen screamed. "I said I wanted them alive!"

Time felt like it slowed almost to a stop.

Titania felt dizzy. Shocked. She took to the sky, her wings carrying her even as her arms couldn't. Everything was blurry.

She saw James down below. He was saying something to her, but she couldn't tell what.

Everything was getting dark. It was hard to breathe. She felt like she was burning up. Everything was heat and light and weightlessness.

The last thing she heard was a distorted, enraged roar like nothing she had ever heard before.

CHAPTER THIRTY-SEVEN

"Titania!" James cried, trying to warn her.

Silen had that snake curled up behind his back. He was sure she couldn't see it. She needed to get out of there! He started running, his legs going faster than he ever thought possible.

Then the snake struck.

James felt like he was sinking into sand. He watched helplessly as Titania flew into the sky. He'd never seen the flames on her body so bright. It was as though she was a supernova about to burn out.

"Titania!" James cried, looking up at her. "Please, don't leave me!"

Her body gave off a bright flash, as bright as the sun, before she started falling. James ran to catch her, but she broke up, disintegrating into ash and embers.

He held his hands out, catching what he could.

A single tear rolled off of his cheek, mixing with her ashes.

He looked up at the darkening sky, his skin transforming into the beast he had been created to be. Dark wings unfurling, the teeth of a lion gleaming. He let out a roar as deep as the ocean before unleashing his fury.

CHAPTER THIRTY-EIGHT

Luna froze as a lion's roar pierced the air. The bear child she had been fighting took the opportunity to bolt into the woods.

She turned to see the ashes falling from the sky.

Titania.

Her heart sank. There was no way.

Luna watched as James completed the morph from a human twisted with grief into a large, winged lion.

They'd gotten him, too.

The handlers were closing in on him, their new prize. She had to do something. Luna rushed forward on her injured legs. James mounted an attack before she could reach him, raising himself up with his wings.

She turned her head, unable to stomach what was unfolding.

In the corner of her eye, she caught a glimpse of Silen as he escaped toward the woods.

No.

He would pay for his crimes. She would not let him get away.

Luna bounded toward the woods, passing the deceased snake on her way. Its head was charred beyond recognition. That was what it got, she thought, for killing Isaac and Titania.

She caught Silen by the ankle a few feet into the forest, sinking her teeth into him. It was satisfying, but she didn't want to kill him. She had other plans for him. He gave out a strangled cry before pitching backward as she drug him to the front of the compound.

When they broke through the other side of the woods, she saw James in lion form padding toward Titania's ashes. The enemies had been defeated.

Luna spotted Natalie underneath a bush at the right side of the compound, with Miranda right behind her. Trevor came slithering around the other side, a few slashes in his ribs. They converged on James, forming a half-circle behind him. What an unusual band they made, Luna thought. A wolf, a giant lizard, a cat, a mouse, and a lion with wings.

James' wings curled in, shrinking as they went. His fur shriveled and his body contorted as he returned to human.

His hands shook as he gathered up Titania's ashes. James curled over them as rain pelted them from the angry sky. His body shook with sobs.

Luna left Trevor in charge of Silen, which Trevor was only happy to oblige. He growled at the now-terrified Silen, daring him to try to run.

Luna trudged over to Isaac's crumpled eagle body, slinking down onto the wet ground herself. She picked him up, having transformed to human to use her own two hands, and found herself unable to hold back the tears anymore either.

The rain could wash away the evidence of what had happened here, but they would never forget.

CHAPTER THIRTY-NINE

James sat, staring out the two-story window, watching the raindrops race down. Fitting, he thought, that it was raining on the anniversary of her death. The cold of the window soaked into his skin. He welcomed it. Welcomed the numbness. He was starting to accept the fact that it might be all he would ever feel again.

A knock at the door jarred him out of his thoughts. He pocketed the blue stone he had been fidgeting with and walked over to open it. Luna stood, folding up a black umbrella.

"Hey," she greeted him, stepping inside and placing the umbrella just beside the doorway to dry on the welcome mat.

"Hey," he said.

He wasn't sure what else to say.

Over the last year, all she had done was try to push him to be part of the crew. To take part in something other than lying about. To move on from Titania's death. But he couldn't. Without her, there was nothing to move on toward. He didn't even have Titania to talk to him about how it felt not to be human. It was ironic, both he and Titania had gone through this without one another, all because of Silen.

He'd be a deadman if it wasn't for Luna. She had said he might be useful, to the point she was willing to fight James over it. And James was done fighting.

He tried his hardest to forget that he wasn't human anymore, but Luna was the exact opposite. She embraced it, almost as though she were proud of it. James couldn't understand that. And he didn't want to. He didn't understand how anyone would willingly embrace this.

Luna shifted nervously from one foot to the other. When she saw the dirty dishes on the counter, she set to work. James' cheeks flushed red. He was going to get to those. He just hadn't felt up to it yet.

"You don't need to do those," James protested, walking to her side.

"It's no trouble at all," Luna said, giving him a faded smile. "I haven't felt up to much the last few days myself. I get it."

James wanted to argue. She hadn't lost Adam, after all.

But he didn't. Because even though she hadn't lost the person she loved the most, she had suffered a loss nonetheless. There was no point in comparing. James felt bad that Isaac had died trying to rescue him. He hadn't asked for that. He didn't know how to process it all.

"I just came to check in and see if you wanted to join Adam and me," Luna said nonchalantly. "We are going to put flowers on Isaac's honorary grave."

They had buried Isaac's eagle body a few miles from the compound where everything had gone down, just after setting the other six Titans free. But, since they wouldn't be traveling back that way, Luna had gone into the sanctuary city's graveyard and made him a memorial there. She visited it regularly, but James had only been once or twice.

They hadn't made one for Titania.

James winced, looking over to the mantle where she sat. Well, what remained of her.

Her ashes were housed in a small urn. Luna had helped James gather them up when... when she died.

"Hey," Luna said, touching his shoulder gently. "If it's too much, you don't need to come. I just thought I'd offer."

James nodded, mulling it over. A gust of wind shook the window in the living room. The storm outside seemed to get more volatile.

"I'm gonna stay in. But if you're going to go, you'd better get a move on," James recommended. "Before this turns into a flood."

"Alright," Luna said, defeated. She gave him a hug, which he hadn't been expecting. He looked down at the top of her blonde hair, awkwardly hugging her back and patting the top of her head.

"Be safe," he told her as she opened the door.

"Thanks." He could barely hear her voice over the downpour.

She popped the umbrella open and reached to close the door, but the wind got to it before she did. The gust violently slammed it shut, causing the entire apartment to shutter.

James didn't think much of it until he turned around and saw the urn teetering on the edge of the mantle. He rushed to it to catch it before it fell, bounding over the couch and knocking his cup of peppermint tea off the end table.

His hand reached out to grasp the urn right as it contacted the ground. The bottom shattered. Ashes spilled out into his hand and onto the floor.

James sat, gathering them up into his hands. He couldn't help it. Tears started rolling down his cheeks.

She was really gone. And he was all alone, sitting on the floor of an apartment, crying into her ashes like a big baby.

James wept, his shoulders shaking as his tears spilled onto the ashes.

He felt the ashes get heavier. That was strange. He opened his eyes fully, trying to clear the tears.

Caught as though by an unfelt gust, the ashes flew into the air and began taking form. Titania's body materialized out of the blue, the ashes swirling around until each and every limb was fully formed.

James' breath caught in his chest. He could hardly believe his eyes!

He didn't dare move. A single breath made her chest rise and fall. Her skin wasn't burning anymore, even as he held her. Was this a dream? Had he lost his mind? She opened her eyes, blinking lazily at him.

James leaned in, looking into her eyes, then to her lips. He pulled her in, gently grazing her lips with his. She took a deep breath, relaxing into him. For a moment, the last year didn't exist. It didn't matter. It wasn't real. All that was real was this moment in time.

She was here.

Titania placed a hand on his right shoulder and the other behind his ear, grinning against his kiss. He reluctantly pulled away, stroking her right hand. In that moment, his mind knew the truth of what and who she was.

She'd risen from her ashes. Like a phoenix.

"James?" Titania said, her voice a bit strained.

"Yes?" he said, still captivated by her.

"I, um…" she nervously reminded him with a gesture that her clothing hadn't been fireproof.

James turned as red as a beet. "Of course!"

He fumbled for the blanket on the couch and draped it around her.

"Thanks," she said, her cheeks flushing.

"We've got a lot to catch up on," he said, holding her to his chest.

"I've missed you, Princess."

CHAPTER FORTY

ONE YEAR EARLIER

Brandon leaned over the gaping hole where a door once sat in the Superintendent's office. He had begun to think that, perhaps, he had come underprepared for this.

"James?" He called down.

No response. Just like the transponder over the last day.

He put on his night-vision goggles and descended into the bunker.

Brandon looked around, his heart sinking. James wasn't here. He wasn't anywhere in the building.

Had he been too late?

The door to the bunker lay on the floor, melted in several spots. At first, he mistook them for welding marks. But something seemed off.

He leaned in closer. The burns were in the shape of handprints…

What had done this?

Adrenaline coursed through him. Something was wrong. Very, very wrong.

He bounded out of the bunker and raced to the entrance. If anything could tell him what happened here, it would be the punch-out panel.

Brandon tapped the screen with shaking hands, his breath visible in the cold air. He tapped the menu, selected motion detection photos, and began scrolling through.

The last photo was of him entering the building. The two before that were of James running in and out of the door. And the one before that...

A flaming girl with wings.

Thank you so much for reading this book! If you enjoyed it, please give it a rating on Amazon and share it with a friend.

Turn the page to get a sneak peek of Geneshifters Book Two: Head Under Water

HEAD UNDER WATER

CRASH

Melody jumped, startled by the noise. She was so sleepy and warm in her tank, it was hard to open her eyes. What could be causing such a ruckus?

She unfurled her scaly blue tail and stretched, pressing her arms into the water above her. She forced her eyes open, fighting against their desire to droop.

Had another experiment escaped the grasp of their handler? It was always an exciting day when that happened! She always felt a pang of jealousy when they did. She didn't have that option.

Whatever the scientists had done to her had made her lungs dependent on water. She could no longer inhale air without feeling like she was suffocating. She was confined to her tank, no matter how much she wished she could leave.

Melody pressed her hands to the cylinder's glass, peering out into the lab.

She couldn't see anything! A white smoke seemed to encase the entire room. It was so thick, Melody instinctively held her breath. But then remembered she didn't need to. The smoke wouldn't fill her lungs. She wouldn't feel the sting in her throat and the watering of her eyes. For once, she was glad to be on this side of the glass. Under the water.

Had the crazy scientists dropped something to cause this foggy atmosphere?

A figure emerged from the haze, walking straight up to her tank.

Melody swam to the back of the tank in fright as the figure cupped their hands over their eyes and peered in at her. Their eyes were covered by goggles that made them resemble a bug. She saw what seemed to be a filter over the person's mouth. Were they responsible for the fog?

The figure looked her up and down. She wanted to shiver, but held it in. The intruder coiled their hand back and slammed it into the top of her tank, causing it to crack.

No, no, no!

The water escaped the tank as a little trickle until the figure leveled another hit.

What was she going to do? She couldn't breathe air anymore!

Coming in 2022…

Sign up to be notified for the release of Geneshifters Book Two: Head Under Water on **rebeccalemke.com**

Acknowledgments

I have so many people to thank for helping me make this book a reality.

First. my husband, Thomas. He encouraged me to finish this project despite the many obstacles we faced in the five years I've been working on it. His dedication and assistance is the only reason that the manuscript exists today in its whole, finished form.

Dayn Russell Leonardson, my audiobook producer. The title of audiobook producer hardly is adequate to describe what he brings to the table. His energy, hype, and insane talent have made this book a work of art.

My dragon-gifter, Samuel C, whose support allowed me to acquire all of the first three book covers in the Geneshifter series without worry or strain. I cannot say thank you enough.

My alpha readers, Cody, Erin, and Jared, who all read the very, very rough first draft of this book. Their support and early feedback allowed this book to be the best it could be.

Deranged Doctor Designs for their amazing work on the covers in this series. There was a reason I had working with them on my bucket list, and I couldn't be happier to have gotten the chance.

Finally, a big thank you to everyone who is helping with the launch of this book, leaving reviews, and telling their friends!

ABOUT THE AUTHOR

Rebecca Lemke is an author, artist, and yarn addict. When she's not writing or sewing, she's chasing her little one around their Oklahoma farm house with her husband, Thomas.